Finna

FINNA

NINO CIPRI

A TOM DOHERTY ASSOCIATES BOOK

NEW YORK

FINNA

Cover art by Carl Weins
Cover design by Christine Foltzer

Edited by Carl Engle-Laird

A Tor.com Book
Published by Tom Doherty Associates
120 Broadway
New York, NY 10271

www.tor.com

Tor® is a registered trademark of
Macmillan Publishing Group, LLC.

ISBN 978-1-250-24572-4 (ebook)
ISBN 978-1-250-24573-1 (trade paperback)

First Edition: February 2020

For my grandmothers. I miss you.

Finna

CHAPTER ONE

The bus abandoned Ava on the outskirts of LitenVärld's vast parking lot, nearly three-quarters of a mile from the doors. The box store stuck out like a giant square pimple on the landscape, which had been scraped into gently undulating drifts of snow by February's wind. Ava marched grimly toward the exterior, painted a cheery sky-blue and sunflower-yellow. The parking lot was mostly empty; it was a Tuesday and the weather was shit. Who would want to go shopping today?

"Fucking Derek," she muttered into the wind, cursing the coworker who'd called in sick. If the world were even the slightest bit fair, she'd be home in bed, alternating Netflix binges with long intermissions to listen to Florence and the Machine and actively feel like shit. That's what she wanted from her days off: equal time to nourish her heartbreak and distract from it. That's all she'd been doing since she broke up with Jules, three days before.

LitenVärld was the bastard offspring of more popular big box stores, hanging in the margins between home goods giants and minimalist furniture mavens. It compromised between clean Scandinavian design and bougie Americana by selling furnishings that displayed neither virtue. Instead of sections, the store ushered shoppers through an upsetting and uncoordinated procession of themed showrooms, which bounced from baroque to postmodern design. The showrooms sat next to each other uneasily, like habitats in a hyper-condensed zoo. Here was the habitat for the Pan-Asian Appropriating White Yoga Instructor, complete with tatami mats and a statue of Shiva; next to it huddled the Edgelord Rockabilly Dorm Room, with black leather futon and Quentin Tarantino posters.

Ava made her way to Her Majesty's Romper Room, a princess-themed play area, which had a doorway to the break room and time clock. It gave Ava a headache if she paid too much attention as she walked through the store, even using the shortcuts only staff knew about. The best she could do was to shut off her peripheral vision and focus only on her goal.

Maybe Jules won't show up today, Ava thought as she squeezed past the gaudy miniature throne. Ava had told Jules that she needed space, and had changed her schedule so that she wouldn't have to see them at work. Jules had listened grimly, then shrugged and said, "I'm not going to fight over territory I don't want to be in anyway. I hate that place."

Ava wasn't quite willing to hope that they'd gotten fired, but a generalized wish that Jules wouldn't be at the store? That felt okay. They were already on their last excused absence for the quarter; maybe they'd just quit.

Ava clung to that thought—that Jules might not be at LitenVärId today—hating that it brought her so much comfort. She clocked in, dumped her stuff in her locker, and got ready to go out onto the floor. She would have had to come back here anyway on Tuesday. She could do this.

As she turned the corner out of the break room, Ava collided with her ex.

"Crap, sorry," Jules said, sounding distracted. Then Jules caught sight of who they were talking to, and froze. "Ava? What are you doing here?"

Jules had brought the cold in with them, ice clinging to their jacket and the thin ends of their twists, melted snow coursing down their brown skin. They smelled like wet wool and Old Spice, which had always been improbably attractive. Ava backed out of the danger zone, back into the smell of stale coffee and ancient crusts of food splatter from the microwave that emanated from all break rooms.

"I got called in," Ava said. "Fucking Derek is sick."

Jules looked panicked. Ava felt bad for them; she'd

been prepared for this to happen, and they hadn't.

"It's just for today," she added.

"Okay," Jules said. They were visibly pulling themself back together. "I'm just gonna—"

The two of them did that annoying dance forced on any two people who wanted to get past each other in a narrow space. Finally, Ava backed all the way against the wall, waving Jules past her.

"Look, just go," she snapped.

Jules opened their mouth to snap back, then shut it and moved past her. As they did, Ava caught sight of the scarf around Jules's neck; light green dotted with blue, brown, and gray, crocheted with thick yarn. She'd made it for Jules for Christmas. In retrospect, the project had sprung from a desperate hope that the two of them might come together again, stitch fragile connections over the yawning holes opening up between them.

"Is that . . . ?" she asked, gesturing.

Jules looked puzzled, then glanced down with a tense grimace. Jules's emotions were always written clear on their face, and they looked like they'd found a snake wrapped around their neck.

"Never mind," Ava said, and fled down the hallway, onto the shop floor.

• • •

Ava volunteered for shifts at the customer service desk with Tricia, their manager, to keep far away from Jules in stocking and assembly. Heartache felt like a persistent hangover: lethargy, a headache, an unshakeable belief in the cruelty of the world, drifting outside of time. It was hard to keep up the bullshit facade of industriousness when she felt entirely dead inside. The minutes dragged by as Ava attempted to look busy while Tricia hovered behind her.

A young woman with olive skin and thick, black-brown hair approached the desk, and Ava turned toward her desperately. "Good morning," she said, trying to inject some cheerfulness into her voice—mostly for Tricia's benefit. Ava thought she sounded strangled.

"Hi," the woman said. "I'm sorry to bother you, but I think I lost my grandmother."

"Lost her?" asked Ava.

"She was right behind me in the showrooms? I turned around to get her opinion, and she was gone. I've been looking for her for ten minutes and ..." She trailed off, shrugging helplessly. Ava turned to find Tricia, then flinched back when she saw the manager already looming behind her. She hadn't even heard Tricia approach.

"I'm so sorry to hear that," Tricia said gravely. She had donned one of her Managerial Faces that Jules had reportedly seen her practicing alone in her office: Calm

And In Charge. She tilted her head, the blond highlights in her midwestern manager-class haircut catching the light. "Let me make an announcement over the PA system. What's her name?"

"Ursula," the young woman replied. "Ursula Nouri."

Tricia nodded, her face serious as she picked up the phone and pressed a button. Her voice came squawking out of the overhead speakers. "Good morning, shoppers. Would Ursula Nouri please meet her party at the customer service desk? Ursula Nouri to the customer service desk, please."

Ava tried to smile reassuringly at the young woman. Tricia treated everything with the gravity usually reserved for state funerals and hostage negotiations.

Tricia set the phone back down in the cradle. "Can you tell me what your grandmother was wearing?"

The girl nodded. "She had on a red coat and some purple fleece gloves. Oh, and a leather purse. I've got a picture of her, if that helps?"

Tricia and Ava dutifully looked at the picture the girl pulled up on her phone. Ursula looked like a fairly average grandmother: white hair pulled into a low bun at the back of her neck, a billowy shirt hanging over a plump frame. The picture was obviously a selfie of Ursula and her granddaughter, the two of them smiling identically up at the camera.

"She seems nice," Ava ventured.

"She is. I mean, she'll tell you when your cleavage is hanging out or your boyfriend is trash, but..." The woman trailed off, staring harder at the small screen. After a moment, more words spilled out: "She doesn't normally wander off like this? She knows I get really worried about her, because we're like, the only family we have. It's this whole, stupid, tragic story that I *super* don't want to get into right now, so if you could just..."

Ava shot a helpless look at Tricia, who thankfully took charge.

"Ava, go through the showrooms and see if you can find her. I'll send a couple of other people up there to look with you. Miss, why don't you wait with me?"

Ava nodded. As she walked past the young woman, she hesitated. "I'm sure she's fine," she said.

The woman's face cracked into an uncertain smile. "Thanks."

. . .

The showrooms were eerily empty. The customer service desk was located at the central hub of the store, and even on slow days, it tended to bustle. The rest of the store felt abandoned, besides a few desultory shoppers and a pair of teenagers alternately making out and taking selfies in the Pastel Goth Hideaway. Then again, it was the downseason, a stark contrast to the roiling hell that had been six weeks prior to Christmas. And sure, it was hard to leave the house in February. Ava had suffered enough coming to LitenVärld today, and she was paid to be here. Still, it was odd to see all the fake apartments vacant; it reminded Ava of the haunting feeling of being the last one out of the store. Each showroom was like an empty home, waiting for its ghostly inhabitants to return.

Or maybe the inhabitants had never left, but were just hiding out, watching the interlopers pass through their abodes.

"Get it together," Ava told herself. Could she blame her paranoia and morbid thoughts on the heartache? Or maybe she should blame it on February. The shortest month, and objectively the worst.

LitenVärld was laid out like a twisting vine, with showrooms branching off a central walkway that wound through the store, curving back on itself before dumping people out into the food court and registers. Ava made her way quietly down the path, peering into the cubes for Ursula Nouri. Each room was alien and strange relative to the one before it. Strung together, they resembled an ugly necklace designed by a child, picking out the most garish beads to thread.

That familiar sense of disorientation came over Ava,

that slight queasiness at seeing all these clashing rooms squeezed together. It mixed with her dread and made her stomach churn. She turned a corner, saw a tall figure in the middle of the Nihilist Bachelor Cube, and let out a shriek before she realized it was Jules.

"Fuck!" Jules shouted, colliding with modular shelves stacked with Camus and Palahniuk novels. "What the hell! Why are you screaming at me?"

"Sorry!" Ava said. Her fright was quickly transmuting to irritation, as all her feelings seemed to do when Jules was concerned. "You startled me."

"I startled you?" they asked incredulously. "I'm not the one sneaking up behind people and screaming like a Nazgûl. God, I almost pissed myself."

They had a fist pressed to their chest, like enough pressure would slow down their pulse.

"Sorry," Ava said again, the word sour in her mouth. Seemed like too many of her conversations with Jules had required apologies. "Did Tricia send you to look for the missing grandmother?"

"I volunteered. A soccer mom enlisted me to help harangue her husband into shelling out money for a new bathroom vanity. She managed to misgender me four times in two minutes," Jules said. They bent down to pick up the books they'd knocked off the shelf. "Two different pronouns, completely ignored my nametag, eventually settled on calling me 'the kid.'"

"Have you seen the old woman?" Ava asked, cutting off Jules's nervous rambling. "The granddaughter says she disappeared around here."

Jules shook their head. "I've been through all the rooms back there," they said, waving their hand the opposite way Ava had come. "Didn't see anything."

"Shit," Ava said. Where could an old woman escape to in a furniture store? She leaned against a showroom wall to think.

"I still think this is the most depressing showroom," Jules said conversationally. "It reeks of misogyny and sadness."

The Nihilist Bachelor's room was one of the smallest show apartments. Tiny kitchenette, a fold-out desk beneath a loft bed, fake exposed brick along the walls. A single brown leather chair in front of a flatscreen TV. Ava thought briefly of Jules's studio, which wasn't much bigger, but was infinitely more comfortable. Jules had refused to buy anything except a set of plates from Liten-Värld, and had furnished it from estate sales and Goodwill trips instead. *Everything at work is part of a set with everything else,* they'd explained. *I don't fit into any of those sets.*

Ava realized that they'd been standing and staring at each other. She turned on her heel and said, "Maybe she wandered into housewares."

"Am I that awful to be around?" Jules asked. There was something raw in their question; something flushed and bruised, radiating hurt. "You can't even stand being in the same room as me. I thought you wanted to be friends."

Had she said that? Probably. That's what you were supposed to say when you ended a relationship with someone you couldn't hate, but didn't know how to love, either.

"Please don't be so dramatic about this," Ava said, trying to keep her voice cool.

"Me?" Jules said. "You switched your entire schedule around so you'd never have to see me again. And you're calling me dramatic?"

"I think it's reasonable to want some space!" If it was so reasonable, some distant, detached part of her wondered, why was she so defensive?

"You're acting like a stranger, or like I don't exist, like we never—"

"So what, you think I'm just *overreacting*?" Ava spat. It was one of the accusations that had stung her the most. She was emotionally volatile. She made mountains out of molehills. She couldn't control her feelings. She'd never claimed otherwise, she'd just stopped being able to fake it around Jules.

Jules opened their mouth to answer, then snapped it

shut. "I'm not gonna do this with you in this stupid room," they said, and turned to go.

"*This* is why I changed my schedule," Ava hissed at their back.

Jules suddenly stopped, and Ava felt her hackles rise. Was this it? A rehash of the fight, their last fight, which was just the same as every fight?

"Ava," they said instead. And there was something in their voice that cut through the fight-or-flight haze: something low, confused, vulnerable. They said her name like they were reaching for a life jacket.

"What?" she replied. Still on guard, but putting away her guns.

"Weren't we in the Bachelor Cube?"

What kind of question was that? But Jules's uncertainty infected her. She glanced to the right; *Fight Club* and *The Stranger* were still on the bookshelf. "Yeah?" she said. "So?"

Jules slowly turned around. "Doesn't it look kind of . . . big?"

The Nihilist Bachelor Cube—like its cousins Coked-out Divorcée, Parental Basement Dweller, and Massage Therapist Who Lived in Their Studio—were all two hundred square feet or smaller, with an open floor plan to make each feel less claustrophobic. Jules had stomped into a separate room that shouldn't have existed, a room

Ava hadn't seen from the walkway. Its design was radically different: bright, colorful, filled with floral prints and fake plants, posters of fantastic places on the wall. It resembled the Midlife Crisis Mom room, but that was on the other side of the store, and had been painted a warm peach color. This one was done in sand and cerulean.

Past the edges of the cube, Ava could see a whole other walkway, one that shouldn't exist. Her gaze traveled up, and she gasped as she saw a seam connecting the two rooms. It was a dark purple, the color of a fresh bruise, and wriggled and squirmed as if it were alive.

"This is weird, right?" Jules said from the other side of the seam. Their voice was normal. Ava had expected it to be warped by passing through the seam.

"This is *really fucking* weird," agreed Ava. She couldn't seem to tear her eyes from that writhing border. It took a moment to hear Jules calling her name.

"What?" she asked.

They held up a pair of purple fleece gloves. "The old woman was wearing purple gloves, right?"

"Shit," Ava sighed. She pulled out the phone on her hip.

"This is amazing," Jules said. "It's a creepy Scandinavian Narnia. I can't believe we found something like this."

"Tricia," Ava said into the phone, and Jules whipped their head around. "We've got a situation up in the showrooms."

"I'll be right there," Tricia replied, and hung up.

"Seriously?" Jules said. They sighed with melodramatic disappointment. "We find a wrinkle in time and you tell the manager?"

"What did you expect me to do?" Ava said. "Will you get out of the . . . whatever that is? You don't know what's in there." That seam between the rooms twitched unpleasantly, and Ava took a step back.

"It can't be much worse than what's back there," Jules said, waving vaguely at Ava, LitenVärld, who knew what.

Jules always wanted to run away. For a long time they'd talked about the two of them leaving together, moving or traveling. The destination changed, but the wanderlust remained the same. The last few weeks, they had more often talked about disappearing on their own. No destination in particular, just . . . away.

"Jules," Ava said urgently, but couldn't think of anything to follow it with. What could she possibly say to bring them back?

Jules sighed, looked down at the gloves in their hand, and then trudged over the threshold. "Ursula had the right idea," they muttered as they passed Ava.

CHAPTER TWO

Tricia called an emergency meeting, and everyone who wasn't working a register crammed into the break room.

It always surprised Ava how many people worked at LitenVärld. She only saw most of them crammed in here during the pre–Black Friday war meeting, or for their exquisitely painful "sensitivity training." She'd only gotten through the latter by focusing on her and Jules's plans to get obliteratingly drunk afterward.

They hadn't even been dating at that point. They'd woken up the next day in Ava's apartment; Jules's shoes had been in the bathtub, while Ava was wearing their shirt. It had smelled like blunts and Old Spice, unexpectedly comforting. Jules was sleeping on the couch, wearing an oversized sweater and a pair of boxers, using Ava's bathrobe as a blanket. She'd stared at them for nearly a minute, trying to piece together the events that had led to her cute new coworker sleeping half-naked on the couch. Eventually, she shook herself out of her daze, told herself to stop being a creep, and went into the kitchen to make coffee. Jules had stumbled in twenty minutes later, wearing the bathrobe they'd slept under, curls flattened on one side. "I will trade you my soul for coffee," they'd said solemnly. Then, when they saw that all Ava had were Nifty! brand beans from PriceLow, they cringed and said, "Those only get part of my soul."

They hadn't hooked up that night, or even that week, but infatuation was already sinking its claws into Ava, catching her bleary and unprepared.

Ava went to the far side of the room, opposite to where Jules was standing. She caught a few whispered conversations between her coworkers, a couple of raised eyebrows, but kept her eyes down. This was the other reason she hadn't wanted to be scheduled with Jules. She hated being gossip fodder. Jules, of course, was impervious to gossip, willfully oblivious. They'd never understood why it irked Ava so much. *People are going to talk,* they always said. *No matter what you do.* Ava had admired their courage at first, but she eventually recognized it as yet another way of shutting people out before they could hurt you.

Tricia finally came in, wheeling a boxy television that looked like it predated LitenVärld itself, or at least this particular store. She plugged it into the wall, then turned to address everyone.

"Can I have some quiet, please?" she called into the already quiet room. After a few seconds, she said, "Thank you. So for anyone that hasn't already heard, we've got a maskhål."

There was a swell of dismayed groans and whispers. Ava, almost unwillingly, found herself seeking out Jules. They had done the same, and mouthed, *A what?*

"Quiet, please," Tricia said again. "And please hold all of your questions until the end. For the benefit of those who've joined us since our last maskhål, I'm going to play a short instructional video."

Another groan, this one softer and more hushed. Tricia didn't even bother to shush anyone, just bent over and pressed play on . . . was that a VHS player?

The video began with a click and a whir. Static flickered in lines across the screen, then cleared, but the color was still slightly off, oversaturated and alien.

Yellow letters traveled across the screen, marquee style: *Maskhål och du.* Below it, in subtitles, "WORM-HOLES AND YOU."

The LitenVärld logo appeared at the bottom of the screen as a man and woman walked into the shot. Judging by their hair and fashion, this video had been made before Ava was born. They both wore polo shirts in LitenVärld's signature sky-blue, with yellow and crimson accents, tucked into unflattering khakis with pleats where no pleats should ever be. Their hair didn't seem to move, stuck in helmet-like structures to their scalps, which made the rest of their faces look weirdly mobile.

Their voices were overdubbed. Badly.

"What's up, amigos?" said the pallid white man. His voice was a cross between Wolf of Wall Street and California beach bum. "I'm Mark!"

"And I'm Dana," warbled the blonde.

"Is Dana drunk?" Ava whispered to one of her coworkers. The coworker rolled his eyes and didn't say anything. (God, they were all so *boring*. She'd forgotten how this store sucked the life from people.)

Mark spoke again. "We're here to tell you what to do if a wormhole opens up on your shift!"

Mark spoke in exclamation points. His voice was far more energetic than the actor, who was wan, bland in that vaguely Scandinavian way, an off-brand Mads Mikkelsen with all the interesting bits filed off.

"First, we should get our disclaimer out of the way," Dana said, in her wobbly, nasal whine. She had an affected mid-Atlantic accent, like she was auditioning for a minor role in *Breakfast at Tiffany's*. The original actress moved with the confidence and poise of a piece of seaweed washed ashore. "LitenVärld accepts no responsibility or liability for any losses or injuries that wormholes incur, since they fall under the Act of God clauses on our employee insurance. This training video does not replace the longer and more in-depth training for our FINNA division—"

Tricia bent over and skipped ahead on the video, speeding through what looked like several more minutes of banter and/or legalese. "The FINNA divisions were made redundant during the Recession. Each store handles the maskhål in-house now."

She restarted the video on a close-up of Mark. "—that's out of the way, it's time for a short physics lesson. In physics, the term *quantum entanglement* refers to particles that are linked in strange ways that we don't entirely understand, but that we can measure."

Mark's pallid face with its receding hairline faded into a cheesy animation. Two blobs appeared on the screen: one a dusky pink, the other a sky-blue. Ava could guess what was coming next, but that didn't stop the physical pain of watching it happen. The pink blob grew eyes with heavy lashes, two spots of reddish purple appearing on what could generously be called its cheeks. The blue blob also grew eyes, along with a heavy brow and—god save them all—a handlebar mustache.

Then the two blobs began *flirting*—cooing and blowing kisses at each other. It was the most obnoxiously heterosexual thing Ava had seen since the last St. Patrick's Day parade.

"Even across vast distances of space and time . . ." Dana said in a dreamy voiceover.

The two blobs were torn away from each other, flung to opposite sides of the screen with a crude galaxy projected between them. *Good,* Ava thought savagely, as the blobs squeaked in distress.

" . . . entangled particles find ways of reconnecting," intoned Dana, and the two blobs snaked out long, ghostly limbs toward each other, joining hands across the galaxy. The two blobs burbled happily, and Ava rolled her eyes.

"This video is making me gayer out of spite," Jules muttered, clear even from the other side of the room.

Ava snorted. She couldn't help it. Jules turned toward her in surprise, and she cleared her throat and turned away.

"Quiet, please!" Tricia said.

On the screen, the obnoxiously heterosexual blobs had been replaced with the vapidly heterosexual actors. They relaxed in a retro LitenVärld showroom—Newly Retired Swinger, Ava would call it. It was done up in beige and mauve tones, with some palm tree and flamingo accents to keep it from being too bland.

"You may be wondering what this has to do with the wormhole in your store," Mark said. The actors' mouths always kept on moving for seconds after the end of the dub, which was giving Ava a headache.

Dana addressed the camera head-on. "Some scientists believe in the *many worlds theory.*" She pronounced it as if it were something strange and exotic, not three words that could come up by themselves in any conversation.

The blue-and-crimson logo on-screen shivered and split into two parts. Mark spread his arms, fingertips extended, augmenting the physics lesson with jazz hands. It was embarrassing to watch him try to emote.

"This means that there are an infinite number of universes," Mark said. "Endless varieties of them. That means that there are endless varieties of LitenVärlds!"

Dana and Mark snapped their fingers. Suddenly, they were sitting in two entirely different rooms; hers was a lavish, baroque French drawing room, and she wore the gown and powdered wig to match. Mark sat in a room that might have been considered "futuristic" when the video was made: lots of neon, inflatable furniture, and one of the largest and ugliest desktop computers Ava had ever seen. He was wearing wraparound sunglasses, a puffy orange vest, and fingerless gloves.

Mark took off the sunglasses and continued. "The unique layout of LitenVärld encourages wormholes to form between universes. These wormholes connect our stores to LitenVärlds in parallel worlds."

Mark and Dana looked at each other, then snapped their fingers again. Now Mark stood in a rustic log cabin, wearing lederhosen and carrying an ax. Dana relaxed in a beach house, wearing a sarong over a bathing suit and holding a daiquiri in her hand.

"That is *not* how physics works," Jules muttered. Why was it so easy to always catch their voice?

Tricia bent over to fast-forward the video again. "It goes on for a while," she said. "You all get the idea."

They watched Mark and Dana flicker through a series of settings and costumes, some of them benign or bizarre, others straight-up racist. Dana in a teahouse and an exaggerated geisha getup got a couple of disgusted sighs, but Mark in a hut and with fake black dreadlocks and a bone through his nose earned widespread groans, and someone (probably Jules) threw a wadded-up paper at the screen. Not even Tricia could say anything about that.

The bizarre zoetrope of Marks and Danas ended with the two actors in foam dinosaur costumes. They attempted to snap their fingers again, fumbling with their thick, rubbery claws, but the sound effect was apparently enough to bring them back to their original world, original bodies. They both heaved affected sighs of relief.

"Now," Mark said, putting his hands on his hips. "Before you decide that traveling to other universes is all fun and games, we should warn you that not all LitenVärlds are as nice as the one *you* work in."

Dana added, "Here's some footage taken by one of our FINNA divisions during recoveries."

Ava's eyes grew wide at the shaky, grainy footage that blasted across the screen. It was hard to make out the details, but Ava caught glimpses of something enormous, something with far more legs than a sane universe could ask for. There were shouts and screams in what a distant, shocked part of Ava's mind guessed was Swedish. A spray of blood hit the camera, and the footage cut out.

Back to Mark and Dana in the bland Retired Swinger living room. Ava broke out into goosebumps when she saw their smiles again.

"Now that you understand what wormholes are, and what might lay on the other side of them, we're going to tell you what to do in case one opens up in your store," Dana said.

Mark leaned forward. "After alerting your manager to the presence of a wormhole, the first and best thing to do is rope off the affected area. Make sure that no customers or associates enter it. They'll usually collapse on their own within a couple hours."

"The only time you need to worry is if someone accidentally wanders into the wormhole. Since 1989, all LitenVärld stores have been equipped with the FINNA, a patented piece of equipment that can locate lost people using quantum entanglement. It helps the FINNA division in your store navigate the series of wormholes that the lost person may have wandered through. In our experience, wormholes tend to travel in packs."

A piece of technology popped up on the screen. To Ava, it looked vaguely like the brick phones that bankers talked on in movies set in the '80s. It faded into an exploded view, familiar to anyone who had had to put together a piece of furniture from a LitenVärld instruction booklet.

Tricia paused the movie, then shut off the TV. It went black with a quiet pop. "As I mentioned, the company closed its FINNA divisions back in 2009, as a cost-saving measure. Instead, I'll need two volunteers who are willing to take the store's FINNA and go after the missing woman."

The room went silent, as every employee became intent on disappearing. Ava shrunk down in her seat and avoided Tricia's eyes. She felt a momentary pang of guilt, thinking of the young woman who'd reported her grandmother missing. But Ava had no interest in death by . . . by whatever those things had been.

"Are we getting overtime for this?" someone else asked.

Ava glanced up long enough to see Tricia shake her head. "Not unless you remain in the other worlds past eighty hours in a single pay period. But! I do have a couple of Pasta and Friends gift cards for the brave volunteers."

Ava scrunched down in her chair even further. Nobody in their right mind would volunteer for—

"Jules!" Tricia said, and Ava felt the name go through her like an electric shock. "Thank you for stepping up."

Ava looked over to see Jules with their hand raised. Everyone else in the room was staring too. Jules shrank under the attention, and awkwardly waved before slumping back down in their plastic chair.

"I don't really need the gift card," they told Tricia.

Tricia shrugged. "Well, that just doubles the incentive for the next volunteer. Any takers? Two gift cards would make for a pretty good date night."

If it had been possible to crawl underneath her chair, transform into a literal puddle, Ava would have done it. She hadn't thought she could sit through a worse work meeting than the sensitivity training.

"Well, if nobody volunteers, corporate policy is to have the people with the least seniority go. That's Jules, but since—since Jules has already volunteered, we need someone else to join Jules on this mission."

Ava winced as she listened to Tricia contort her speech in an effort to avoid using they or them. *I just can't do it!* Tricia had cheerfully told Ava once, completely unprompted. *I guess I'm too much of a grammar nazi!* Since then, she went out of her way to avoid using any pronouns at all when talking about Jules, warping her sentences around her refusal. Ava wondered, not for the first time, why anyone would so proudly declare themselves to be any kind of nazi. She was so distracted by her irritation that she missed the last bit of Tricia's speech, and it took her a few seconds to realize everyone was staring at her.

Rewind: The policy was to send the person with the least seniority. That was Jules. Jules had been hired on two months after Ava. Was there anybody else in between them?

Derek. Fucking Derek, who was the entire reason that Ava was here on a day she'd explicitly asked not to work.

"Oh, *hell* no," Ava said.

"Why don't the three of us talk in my office?" Tricia said sweetly.

• • •

Tricia's office was a purgatory of fallen LitenVärld fashions, a claustrophobic island of misfit furniture. Chairs with denim upholstery, a glass-top desk with chrome accents, and a gag novelty lamp in the shape of a hairy, muscular leg, complete with sock garters. The look was completed by a couple of soulless art prints that reminded Ava of waiting rooms in urgent care clinics.

Ava decided to take a reasonable approach, since it was that or run screaming out of the store. "Tricia," she said.

"This is really unfair. I know I don't have the seniority—"

"You do have the right to refuse the assignment," Tricia said.

Relief flooded through Ava. "Okay, in that case—"

"But it would be grounds for termination."

All the relief flooded right back out of her, replaced by a vision of her current checking account balance. "What?!"

"Listen, Tricia," Jules said, leaning forward. "I'm happy to do this by myself. I don't need—"

"Jules, I appreciate your willingness to go above and beyond. It's a nice change from your usual MO." Tricia laughed like the soulless bitch she was. "But we do have to stick to policy, which says that nobody goes through a maskhål alone." Tricia turned her blank gaze back to Ava. "Furthermore, I'd like you both to keep in mind that there's a young woman sitting in the cafeteria who's scared for her grandmother. Customers always come first."

Ava was, possibly for the first time in her life, too angry to speak. If she lived through this, she decided, she was going to track Derek down and kill him.

"Let's get you the FINNA," Tricia said. "Oh! And don't forget these!"

She slid the two gift cards across the table.

CHAPTER THREE

"Okay, so, listen," Jules said.

Ava dropped the box carrying the FINNA on the ground and squatted next to it. Behind them, in the Nihilist Bachelor Cube, the maskhål squirmed in the air. The seam between their world and *another universe* twitched restlessly. Ava turned her back to it, so she wouldn't have to look.

"I'm listening," Ava said, opening the box. The FINNA looked like some of the equipment she'd seen on Ghost Hunters reruns, with a massive gray case, a black-and-green console, and two antennae on the side. It was lighter than it looked, at least.

Jules peered over her shoulder. "The instructions should be in here," they said, plucking the booklet out. "In Swedish, French, and Japanese, great. I can muddle through the French— Or yank them out of my hands, that works too."

"You don't need written instructions, the diagrams are made to be universally understandable," Ava said, flipping to the pictures.

She knew she was acting like a royal bitch, but she was still so angry at Tricia, at her corporate overlords, and at the universe—sorry, the *multiverse*—in general. She tried to rein her irritation in as she said, "What were you going to say before?"

Jules took a deep breath and let it out slow. They'd gotten good at not rising to her bullshit, not taking the bait she waved in front of them. Their discretion hadn't helped; Jules's calm demeanor while Ava lost her shit had just made her feel even angrier. The heart was a stupid, hurting animal, and her heart was stupider than most.

"I know that you don't want to do this," Jules said. "And that I'm the last person you want to do it with. So here's my proposal."

Ava stopped flipping through the diagrams, enough to signal that she was listening.

Jules took a breath. "Go through the maskhål far enough to be out of sight, and chill. I'll find Ursula on my own, and then meet you back there."

The worst part is that she was tempted. Sorely tempted. For a few seconds anyway, before the ever-present anger seeped back in.

"I'm not going to make you wander through a bunch of creepy worlds by yourself," Ava said grumpily. "You can't even follow foolproof diagrams."

"That's why there are instructions."

"It's supposed to be intuitive!"

"It's not intuitive for me!" Jules said. They always lost their patience with Ava eventually, because she could never keep herself from pushing them past their limit. "My brain isn't wired like that, and I don't want it to be!"

Why couldn't Ava keep herself—keep both of them—from getting stuck in these same stupid arguments? "That's why I'm not going to make you explore some weird alternate universe all alone. I don't want you running into whatever the hell those things were in that video," she said, crossing her arms.

"I'd rather face down a whatever-the-hell than constantly hear I'm a screw-up who can't do obvious, simple tasks," Jules said. Their tone was quiet but vehement, full of a subdued anger that cut through Ava's defenses.

"That's not what I think." Had she ever said that? She and Jules had said a lot—a *lot*—of things to each other when they'd broken up, but she'd never . . .

"It's what everyone thinks," Jules said. Their face—normally open, armed with joy and humor—was stony and closed off. "Like doing things my own way is the most ridiculous shit they've ever heard of, even though it's the only way I've ever been happy. Nobody says it to my face, but everyone here treats me like it's a miracle I've gotten this far on my own. I'm on my last warning before I get fired. Tricia would probably be thrilled if I didn't come back."

Ava wanted to deny it, but remembered how often she'd told Jules *this is why we can't have nice things,* in every tone from accusatory to laughing, but most often with that underlying frustration. Jules was so unpredictable, so messy, forever losing or misplacing things, seeming to move in a personal chaos field. It had been thrilling, until it wasn't, until it felt like an extra weight on her own shaky mental health. But she'd never meant to make it seem like Jules should change for her, or for anyone. Especially this stupid job.

"Tricia is garbage anyway," Ava said. "So it's not like her opinion counts for shit."

Jules looked askance at her. "Let's just figure out how this thing works."

Ava spread out the instructions enough for Jules to peer over her shoulder, then tapped one of the diagrams. The diagram pointed to a large bubble on the bottom of the FINNA, like the plastic capsules for vending machine toys. "I'm assuming 'insérez un objet personnel' means insert a personal object?"

Jules wrinkled their nose at Ava's pronunciation. They used to tease her for only knowing English, when they'd grown up speaking English and French, Creole to their Guianan parents and cousins, and knew enough Spanish to crack jokes with the Honduran and Mexican dudes working down in assembly. "You're not wrong," they said begrudgingly. "Just mildly offensive. Here."

They handed over one of the purple gloves they'd found on the other side of the maskhål. Ava pressed a button, and the bubble cracked in half to open. She stuffed the fleece glove into the hollow space, which stretched to accommodate it like hard plastic never could.

"Cool, just gonna not think about how weird that is," she said.

"There should be a switch on the side," said Jules. "Turn it to . . . I guess that's a compass?"

When she did, there was a momentary whine, high-pitched as a mosquito. The glove dissolved into a gently glowing purple haze, trapped underneath the plastic. There was a pleasant ding, like an oven timer, and the console lit up.

"That's so cool," Jules said.

Ava looked back at the diagrams. "I guess we just point it at the maskhål, and it should . . ."

The FINNA beeped cheerfully, and a neon-green arrow appeared on the screen, juddering and moving as she swept the device from side to side. Some of the gauges on the console jumped as she pointed it toward that puckered seam where the two worlds joined.

"I guess that's it," Ava said. The dread that she'd successfully tamped down with anger bloomed in her stomach again.

"I guess so," Jules agreed. They picked up the instructions, put them in their back pocket, then held a hand out to Ava. She wanted to roll her eyes, but she wasn't sure she'd be able to force her leaden legs to move without any assistance.

She let Jules pull her up, and they walked toward the maskhål together.

. . .

The weirdest part about walking through the maskhål was that it wasn't weird at all. Ava had expected to feel something; a membrane, a temperature change, her ears to pop. They took half a dozen steps and were in another world.

It took Ava a few minutes to notice the subtle differences. The world was warmer, a little more humid. The air was fresher in this LitenVärld than in her own. Pastels and paisley seemed to be in fashion in these showrooms, rather than the muted color palettes and natural prints that had dominated this year's catalogue. But there was nothing that screamed *Alien planet! You don't belong here!*

"I really thought another universe would look cooler."

Jules sounded disappointed.

"I guess LitenVärld is the same everywhere," she said. "That's what people want, right? Familiarity?"

"Some people, sure," said Jules. They turned to her. "This place seems chill. You should stay here while I go find Ursula."

Ava rolled her eyes. "I'm coming with you."

"I told you, I can do this on my own," Jules said, frustration bleeding into their tone.

"I know you can!" Ava snapped. It was true. Jules was prepared for anything, everything. They could have been a Boy Scout, if the Boy Scouts weren't transphobic trash. They may have moved in a personal chaos field, but it made them more at ease with the unexpected and strange than anyone. At their best, Jules was good-hearted and calm in emergencies and tended to know what to do. Jules was the person you always, always wanted on your zombie apocalypse team.

"Of everyone in this stupid store," Ava said, "you're definitely the most capable of rescuing someone's grandma from a horde of spider-monsters or whatever were in that video."

"Then why—"

"Because I don't trust you to come back!" Ava hissed. "You always do this. You ignore inconvenient realities like *your girlfriend is fucked up in the head* and *there are gi-*

ant spiders in other worlds! Then when the problems get too big to ignore, you run."

" . . . You dumped *me*," Jules said numbly.

"Because you never would," Ava answered. "I would have just woken up and you'd be gone."

Jules looked like she'd stuck a dagger somewhere soft. Some uncallused piece of them, secreted away from the world and from Jules's own introspection. *You're only with me because you think you can* fix *me,* she'd told them, during that last, caustic fight. *And as long as you're trying to fix me, you don't have to think about all the problems in your own life.* That's the last thing she'd said before Jules had stormed out. The two of them had talked on the phone after, and they'd both apologized for the things they'd said, but neither of them had retracted any of those cruel truths.

Ava, for once, thanked her own cruelty, because it let her keep pushing. "Let me just help, for once. I know I'm mostly useless, but it's too dangerous to go alone."

Jules didn't say anything for long minutes. Ava, hyper-vigilant to disaster, wondered if they were about to yank the FINNA out of her hands and run for it. What would she do? Could she fight them off?

Thankfully, she didn't have to find out. Jules cleared their throat and said, "Which way are we supposed to go?"

Ava relaxed a bit. The arrow on the FINNA's screen had shifted, was pointing them left, toward a large showroom with kitchen tables, astroturf, and fake plants. But when they turned into it, the showroom stretched out into a dizzying, impossibly long room, its end obscured by plants. A warm, humid wind pressed against them. It felt like walking into a gaping mouth.

"Nice," Jules said. Their excitement was faint but palpable. "This is more along the lines of what I was thinking."

Jules stepped into the showroom, and Ava told herself that she had no choice but to follow.

As they walked, the plants grew thicker and distinctly less plastic. The astroturf gave way to real grass, ankle high, dotted with ferns. The ceiling receded, until they couldn't see it past the canopy of plants stretching overhead. The two of them pushed their way through, following the insistent beeps of the FINNA. Ava's shirt stuck to her chest with sweat, her thighs chafing inside her uniform khakis. Eventually, they broke through the thicket of wild plants and into a clearing—they had, at some unknown point, made their way outside. Ava wiped sweat from her forehead as she looked around.

The FINNA led them into what looked like a wild, overgrown orchard planted high up on a hillside. The sun peeked out from behind fat, fast-moving clouds that seemed to race just above the tops of the trees. The trees themselves sprawled low and wide across the grass, with branches that twined into the shapes of chairs and tables. Cookware sprouted up from the ground like sharp, metallic flowers. Two massive butterflies chased each other, each wing the size of a paperback, and with a pattern that looked weirdly like fabric swatches.

"This is amazing," Jules whispered next to Ava. Their voice was hushed, awed. They weren't even out of breath. Ava waved away a cloud of gnats that suddenly descended on her.

"This is weird," she said. "Where is everyone?"

"Who cares? It's gorgeous out here."

It was pretty enough, but Ava was too distracted by the miserable heat to appreciate it. She'd always hated summer. "Can we rest for a second? I feel like I'm going to die."

Ava plopped down in the grass, feeling a vague wave of annoyance toward Ursula Nouri. Why the hell hadn't Ursula turned back once she'd realized she was lost? Then again, maybe she had tried, but gotten increasingly turned around. LitenVärld was disorienting enough without adding in multiple universes.

Jules was running around like a kid at a playground, zooming around and investigating the plants. "This place is amazing. These can't be naturally occurring, right?

They must have been cultivated."

Ava lay back on the grass and closed her eyes. Her nose itched. Great, she was allergic to this new world. Still, the intermittent sun felt good, and there was a fresh breeze drying the sweat that had pooled on her skin. She asked, "If it's cultivated, where are the workers? Where are the customers?"

"Maybe they're permaculture gardens," Jules replied. "Super-casual cultivation. Or maybe this world has moved beyond materialism and the need to keep buying the same crap over and over. Oh my god!"

Ava sat up, ready to run. "What? What is it?"

"Look at these chairs!" Jules called out. "This is *so cool*!"

Ava wanted to throw a clod of dirt at them, but instead dutifully stood up and looked at the chairs Jules was geeking out about. They were bright green wingbacks with purple-red accents, and their fuzzy fabric looked plush and inviting. As Ava got closer, she realized that the chair was covered in gossamer-thin hairs that stood on end, as if at attention. Jules waved their arm, and the bristles seemed to follow the movement, stretching upward toward the limb.

Something caught Ava's peripheral vision, a color that seemed out of place; an artificial crimson that didn't fit in with the lush garden. A scrap of red fabric, just peeking out from a massive, tightly curled bud. She walked over to get a closer look, thinking of Ursula's red coat. Maybe this was another clue. Ava looked down as her foot collided with something. A leather purse.

There was more red on the grass, but not fabric, not a flower. Blood.

"Jules?" Ava said, but her voice had no strength. She turned around, and saw them reaching closer to the chair, toward those wispy bristles that strained upward in return.

Ava had never really had to deal with an emergency; just the slow disaster that was her life. But if that was anything to go by, Ava had always assumed she'd be useless, do the worst possible thing in a horrible situation. But now, she didn't have time to stop and make a decision. She didn't even have time to doubt herself. Her brain shut off, and her body moved in giant steps until she was close enough to grab hold of Jules's shirt and yank them backward.

The wingback chair snapped shut inches from Jules's outstretched fingers. Jules screamed. Ava realized that she'd been screaming the whole time; her throat felt raw, abraded by terror. They stumbled backward, a safe distance from the wingback flytrap.

"Holy shit, that almost killed me," Jules said. They could have been commenting on the weather. "And I'm glad it didn't, but also that is the coolest thing I've ever seen."

Ava socked them in the arm and stomped away.

. . .

Jules knew her well enough to give Ava some time and space. Maybe they had, against all odds, developed a sense of self-preservation. If they had, they could surely tell that she was ready to toss their ungrateful ass into the waiting maw of one of those flytrap chairs. Ava closed her eyes and took deep breaths, trying to will away the tremors and slow her heartbeat. She flinched at a sudden loud clapping sound, opening her eyes and scrambling backward.

It was just Jules, though, sitting a safe distance from the carnivorous wingback chair, and poking at the hairs with a stick.

At Ava's glare, they dropped the stick. "Sorry," they said. Ava turned her back on Jules, grabbed the leather purse, and started going through it.

It was a true grandma bag, roomy and full of all kinds of junk. Ava dug through cough drops, reading glasses, tissues, hand sanitizer, perfume, and several bottles of hand cream before she found a pocketbook. She opened it up: the driver's license read Ursula Nouri, and Ava recognized the woman in the photo from the young woman's selfie.

"It's hers," Ava called out. "Ursula's."

She started flipping through the rest of the pocket-book, mostly out of morbid curiosity. About thirty dollars in cash, some crumpled receipts, a well-used library card, a half-dozen memberships for big box stores like Hearths and Crafts, Hammer City, and, of course, Liten-Värld. Tucked into the same clear plastic sleeve that held Ursula's driver's license, facing the opposite side, was a picture of her with a teenage girl. The young woman at the customer service desk, but years younger. Middle or high school maybe, judging by the acne and the awkward emo outfit that screamed *trying too hard*.

Ava could easily imagine this Ursula dropping some commentary about the skinny plaid pants barely hanging on her granddaughter's hips, and how much eyeliner was too much. Ursula looked a little judgmental, but her arm around the girl was protective, comforting. Ava smiled, then remembered the woman staring at the selfie and saying that her grandmother knew how worried she got.

God, this job sucked.

Jules, never able to leave well enough alone, had progressed to balling up wads of grass and tossing them at the chair. It seemed to be getting wise to their tricks, only half closing when the grass hit the sensitive hairs on what

Ava couldn't help but think of as its tongue. "So she got eaten?" they asked.

Ava looked over at the curled-up plant. The lump was definitely human-sized. "Something is in there. I'm not sure I'm willing to pry it open and find out."

"Yeah," Jules agreed sadly. "That's above our pay grade."

"This whole trip is above our pay grade," Ava muttered. She looked at the FINNA. The arrow in the center of the console still moved as she did, directing her toward something. Oddly, it wasn't pointing at the now-digesting plant. "This thing is still telling us she's out there, though. Piece of crap."

She dropped it and began setting Ursula's purse back to rights. The granddaughter would probably want it back, but she wouldn't miss a couple of cough drops, and Ava's throat was sore from screaming. She popped a cough drop into her mouth and sucked on it.

Jules was squinting at the FINNA's instructions. They liked to talk up their French fluency, but Ava knew that their reading was rusty as shit.

"What color is the arrow in the console?" they called out.

"Yellow?"

"Huh," Jules said.

Ava looked back at them. "What? What is it?"

"It says here that the arrow is green when it locates the exact match of the person being sought. But if that person is indisposed—and I'm guessing they mean *dead*—the light will change to yellow and the FINNA will locate instead . . ."

They trailed off, looking stricken.

"What?" Ava asked. "Locate what?"

Jules closed the booklet. "An appropriate replacement from another universe."

Ava sat up straighter. "Appropriate replacement?"

"That's what it says."

She bellowed, "*Appropriate replacement?!*"

"I am literally just translating."

Ava dropped the FINNA and put her face in her hands. She wanted to scream again, but her throat was still too sore. She crunched the cough drop vindictively.

"This is so fucked up," she said between bites.

"Capitalism," Jules said philosophically.

"Yep." She took her face out of her hands. "So we're supposed to find some alternate universe version of Ursula and bring her back instead?"

"I guess," Jules said, though they sounded conflicted about it. "That's better than coming back empty-handed."

"Is it?" Ava asked. "Is it really? Or is that sorta messed up?"

Jules shrugged. "It's messed up either way. I'm not really in a hurry to go back and tell this girl her grandma is . . ."

They both looked at the Ursula-sized lump in the plant. Ava shuddered.

"Besides," Jules said, "I'd still rather be out here than back in the store and getting grilled on my gender by random customers."

Ava side-eyed them. "You almost got eaten by a chair."

Jules shrugged, and Ava could see the response coming. "What's life without a little risk?"

"You know," she snapped. "I really wish you cared about yourself as much as other people cared about you."

Jules whipped around. "What the hell does that mean? And who the hell are you to say that?"

Ava was caught off guard by the ferocity in their voice.

"You made it abundantly clear that you didn't care about me anymore," they said. "You can't just, just *say* stuff like that when you don't—"

"I care!" She wanted to scream it at them, but all she could get out was a hoarse, broken whisper. "Jules, I—"

The truth was she cared too much, about everything, but Jules most of all. She couldn't stop caring, she felt like she was choking on how much *everything* mattered *so much*. It froze her, or burned her up inside, or sometimes both at the same time in an impossibly cruel alchemy. She'd been diagnosed with depression and anxiety, but really, all it seemed to come down to was this: she cared too much, too often, and it left her oversensitized and insufferable. Jules, when they'd first started dating, had distracted her from how dire everything felt all the time. The sex had distracted her, the dates and the cuddling and the romance. For a while, it had distracted her so completely that she'd believed she was cured. Why hadn't she tried treating her mental health by falling in love with a cute, quirky stranger?

Then she'd started *caring* about Jules. Jules had been absorbed into the cacophony of competing worries and anxieties. She could see that the way she cared about Jules was making them miserable, and her too, but she'd never been able to just disentangle the different kinds of caring. Especially not with Jules.

Damn it, she was crying. She grabbed tissues out of Ursula's purse, hoping they weren't already used as she wiped her face. When her voice was steady enough to speak, she said, "I care. No matter how shit I am at showing it."

"You're definitely shit at that," Jules said bitterly. After a long moment, though, the stiff, angry line of their back relaxed. "But you might be right about some of the other stuff."

They scrubbed a hand over their face. Ava looked away; she knew Jules hated to cry, hated anyone seeing it even more. When Ava cried, her entire face crumpled, her sobs loud brays that broke through her clenched teeth, but at least she felt better afterward. Jules kept their face as still as a statue, and it never seemed to be the same kind of release for them.

They'd given Ava time to calm down, so it was only fair to return the favor. When Jules looked like they were ready, Ava put the purse over her shoulder. "We should go before we're stalked and eaten by a sofa or something. Hopefully the next universe won't try to kill us."

After a brief hesitation, Jules stood up as well. "You've cursed us now."

"Probably," she agreed glumly. The FINNA beeped, directing them toward a dirt path that wound its way through the trees.

CHAPTER FOUR

Walls grew up gradually around them, the dirt path became neat brick, and the plant life began to look more orderly. Ava kept an eye out for the maskhål this time, and spotted it easily. The one in her LitenVärld had seemed to squirm, and was tinted with violet and yellow hues. This seam was thinner, uniform, and seemed . . . stable? Was that possible? Rather than a shifting, moving scar between two worlds, this one looked like it had been reinforced with a honeycomb pattern of lines. It pulsed regularly as Ava watched it, somewhere between organic and mechanical.

The maskhål opened into a recognizable LitenVärld food court, bustling with people. Ava sighed in relief, letting the familiar wave of white noise wash over her: the low murmur of voices, cutlery against plates, footsteps. She wasn't sure she could have dealt with another wilderness, empty except for killer furniture. This LitenVärld looked nearly identical to their own, but the lunch rush was much calmer. No screaming children, no couples arguing over budgets, no amateur interior designers melting down over curtain patterns. It was soothing, exactly what she needed to calm her nerves.

"Do you think this place accepts money from other universes?" she asked Jules. The second she'd smelled the food court, her hunger rumbled through her. But when she turned to look at Jules, she saw that they were hanging back by the wall, eyeing the cafeteria uneasily.

"I don't think we should eat here," they said.

Ava rolled her eyes and handed Jules the FINNA. "You're just mad because nothing is trying to eat *us*."

She got in line. The familiarity was almost as comforting as the thought of getting some food in her belly. She recognized everything from the food court in her own LitenVärld: slices of smoked salmon, potato salad, smörgås arranged in neat, orderly lines, the silver carafes dispensing surprisingly decent tea and awful hot chocolate. Ava got a tray and loaded it up. She paused in front of the desserts, having automatically reached for a plate of the addictive chocolate cake. Her therapist had been yelling at Ava to try and eat at least A Fruit and/or Vegetable A Day. She added an apple from a large glass bowl before moving toward the register.

The apple felt odd in her hands, and she examined it as she waited to pay. It was as round as a tennis ball, red as a fairy tale with bright golden splotches. The splotches looked uniform, evenly dotted around the circumference of the fruit, as if they'd been designed that way. She looked back at the bowl, and saw that the other apples were exactly the same. As if they'd been stamped from the same mold.

Well, it was a different universe, she thought. Just because it felt familiar didn't mean it was the same. Maybe apples in this world were like bananas in her own, identical genetic clones.

"Are you ready, shopper?" the cashier said. Ava looked up and froze.

The woman from the training video was standing behind the register. Dana? Had that been her name? It couldn't have really been her, just someone who bore a creepy resemblance to her. Even though her hair was different—limp blond waves instead of a teased-up helmet—the likeness was uncanny enough to freak her the hell out.

"Shopper?" the woman said. "Are you ready?"

The voice, at least, was different. Ava shook herself and moved her tray up to the register. "Yeah," she said. "Thanks."

"Will this be all?"

Ava nodded. The woman watched her expectantly, the blank smile fading into something suspicious.

"Place your hand on the mortänder, shopper," she said. She gestured to a pad in front of the register. The shape of a hand had been indented into it, and there were small slits interspersed evenly throughout.

Okay, different universe, different rules. Yes, it was creepy, but drawing attention to themselves would be worse, right? Ava hesitantly moved her hand toward the pad, and nearly screamed with fright when someone seized her wrist.

Jules. She snatched her wrist back and hissed, "Don't scare me like that, jerk."

Jules's eyes were on the cashier. "What did you call that thing?"

The woman shifted her unnerving gaze to them.

"It's the mortänder, shopper," she said evenly.

"What's it for?" Jules demanded.

"It's for taking payment, shopper."

"Payment of what?"

Ava was about to elbow Jules and tell them to stop being rude when the woman's reply froze her.

"Why, blood, shopper," she said in an *aren't you silly* voice. Dana nodded to one of the other registers, and *holy shit*, another Dana was standing behind that register, and helping someone who bore a terrifying resemblance to Mark. Mark placed his hand in the mortänder, half-obscured by the tray of food he'd bought. Ava registered, with growing, distant horror, that they'd bought the same food; the smörgås on his tray looked like exact replicas, the chocolate cake and the apple were identical. The sameness was dizzying.

There was a clear *snikk,* a metallic whisper like a blade being drawn. Ava realized that she'd been hearing it this whole time, over and over, but that it had somehow settled into the orderly bustle of the food court. She'd dismissed it as the sound of cutlery. The man's smile twitched, and he drew up his hand.

Blood flowed in bright rivulets down his palm and fingers, spattering across the hand-shaped depression.

"First the mother teeth take the payment. Then Mother's love soothes the hurt," Dana explained.

A thick liquid, like bile, oozed up into the hollow, and the man plunged his hand into it. Red tendrils of blood swirled through the slime until, with a hungry sound, the goo was sucked back down. The man withdrew his hand; the blood was gone, and the cuts had healed into bright pink scars, vivid against his pale skin.

"You're strangers, aren't you?" asked the woman, drawing her eyes away from the blood and goo.

Ava nodded dumbly, before realizing that was probably a bad idea. The man—the Mark, she couldn't help thinking—came over to them. Ava grabbed onto Jules's sleeve, huddling close to them.

"It's been so long since we've had strangers in our hive," Mark said. His voice was nothing like the training video, but it was nearly identical to Dana's in cadence and pitch.

"I wonder why," Jules said faintly.

"We should take them to Mother," Mark said to Dana.

"Let us take them to Mother," Dana said to Mark.

"No, that's okay," Ava tried to say. She felt breathless, her skin was prickling with fear. This was worse, somehow, than the wingback chair.

"Mother will want to meet you."

"Mother will have questions for you."

"Mother will want answers."

Jules pulled Ava back the way they'd come. "We actually have to get going," they said. "We're, uh, on a mission? From our own mother! She sent us here to, uh . . ."

Mark and Dana's faces darkened in awful unison. "Your mother sent you to infiltrate our peaceful hive?"

Ava looked over her shoulder, and felt her stomach drop. They were attracting attention from everyone in the food court. Ava beheld an entire crowd of Marks and Danas, gazing at her and Jules with open hostility.

"No, no," Jules stammered. "That's not what I—what we meant was—"

"Abort," Ava hissed. "Abort!"

"Yeah, fuck this," Jules said. They grabbed Ava's hand, and the two of them ran for it.

So this is what it's like being chased by an angry mob

of clones, Ava thought. *Cool.* This was shock, wasn't it? While she could feel a mute, animalistic terror taking over her body—had she ever run this fast? She hated running, had always walked the last three-quarters of the timed mile during gym class—a part of her brain stood aside and watched, hands on its hips, vaguely bemused.

She followed Jules through the store, showroom cubes blinking past them. The layout was nearly identical to their own LitenVärld's, and she realized that Jules was taking them toward one of the fire exits in the back of the store. It was one of the shortcuts that only employees knew about, or serious LitenVärld shoppers who had memorized the store, followed all the sales, and could order the secret off-menu items in the food courts. Even a stupid place like LitenVärld had a fandom.

They nearly fell headlong into a *giant pit* where the Gen X Family with '80s Nostalgia showroom was supposed to be. Ava had to yank Jules back as they teetered above the pit, which was too dark to see the bottom of. The rising air smelled fetid, like a brackish swamp mixed with dog breath. The sides of it stretched from one side of the walkway to the other, impossible to get around.

"Shit," Jules said. "Shit!"

They tossed the FINNA to their left hand, grabbed a towel rod in their right, and swung it at the advancing group of Marks and Danas. To Ava's surprise, the crowd retreated, backing away and giving them space. Jules looked shocked, like they couldn't believe that had worked.

Ava's wild, trembling hope ebbed as she felt rumbling under her feet. The tremor quaked up through the cement floor, reminding Ava of previous apartments too close to the Metra tracks, or of the tiny earthquake that had woken her once on a visit to family in California.

At the same time, she caught a whisper from the crowd, a growing murmur that seemed to come from everywhere and nowhere at once.

Mother. Mother. Mother. Mother.

"Oh, shit," Ava whispered.

The murmur grew along with the thunderous vibration below, becoming a shout, a chant, an invocation.

Animal panic was taking over now, that last bit of her brain that had been watching in detached irony consumed by the knowledge that *she was going to die.*

Jules fumbled at her hand, and turned Ava toward them, blocking her view of the Marks and Danas shrieking around them.

"Ava, listen," they said, and somehow, the quiet intensity in their voice cut through her panic. "I'm sorry."

Confusion pushed down the noise in her head. "About . . . about the breakup?" she asked. Jules cut their eyes toward the pit.

"Sure, that too," they said awkwardly.

Ava followed their gaze and caught a glimpse of an impossible rend in the air below them, illuminated with a gray-blue light that pulsed along its circumference. A maskhål.

Then Jules shoved them over the edge of the pit.

CHAPTER FIVE

She screamed as she fell, toward the rumbling, through darkness into a sudden burst of light.

She kept screaming right up until she hit the water, hard enough to nearly knock her senseless. She twisted in the water, orienting herself before clawing her way back up toward the surface. She crested the water with a sputtering gasp, dimly aware of Jules doing the same a few feet away.

Once she got her breath back, the first thing she did was send a splash of water right into Jules's stupid face.

"You asshole!" she screamed hoarsely. "You shoved me off a *cliff*!"

Jules coughed out, "I got us away from the horde of retail zombies!"

"They weren't chasing us until you spouted off that garbage about being sent by our own mother!"

"You didn't even notice anything weird until they literally asked you for your *blood*!" they shouted back. "Would you have given it to them? God knows, you do everything else that stupid job asks you to do, even though you hate it."

"At least I wasn't almost eaten by a *chair,* you ass! You're the most impulsive, infuriating—"

"The FINNA led us here!" Jules roared. "It pointed us toward the pit, I saw the wormhole, and I jumped. What would you have done? Agonized about it until they ate us?"

It was true, but that didn't mean she had to accept it. "A warning might have been nice," she pointed out. "Or a quick, 'Hey, there's a wormhole, let's make a getaway.'"

Jules rolled their eyes. "I already apologized, so I don't know what else you expect from me. You're welcome for saving your life, anyway."

They stared at each other in a stalemate. Then Ava realized something.

"Where's the FINNA?"

She was intimately familiar with Jules's *Oh, shit* face, and the bottom dropped out of her stomach when she recognized it flitting across their face. Jules's personal chaos field had struck again.

"You dropped it, didn't you?" she asked.

"Shit," Jules muttered. They looked down into the water, past their feet, searching for it.

"Of course you dropped it," Ava said. She wasn't sure how far they'd fallen, but they'd hit the water *hard.* She would have been more surprised if they'd managed to keep hold of it.

Jules dove down beneath the surface of the water, then came back up. "I can see it!" they said. "I can dive down and get it!"

Ava ducked under the water to look. Far below them, she could see the purple light from the FINNA, its glow barely cutting through the murky salt water.

Ava resurfaced and shoved her hair out of her face. "It's too far," she said. "There's no point—"

But Jules was already taking deep breaths, flooding their lungs and blood with oxygen.

"Jules, don't—!"

But they were gone, disappearing into the murk beneath the surface of the water. Ava looked around. They had landed in a world made of water, flat and gray-skied. The water, at least, wasn't too cold, and it was still as glass, mirroring the clouds above. As the seconds ticked by, Ava became aware of how alone she was. The horizon was impossibly distant.

How long had Jules been underwater? Every time Ava had watched a movie when someone went underwater, she'd instinctively held her breath as well. Now, she felt dread stealing the air from her. "Jules?" she said. Then again, louder, "Jules!"

Nothing. No bubbles broke the surface of the water. No ripples. Nothing moved except for her.

Ava ducked back under the water, ignoring the sting in her eyes as she looked for Jules. But there was nothing in the murk, just the distant, barely visible light of the FINNA. She called out again, remembering distantly that sound carried better in water, "Jules!"

Water splashed into her throat and sinuses, and she pulled herself back above the surface, coughing it out. Why had she yelled at them? Why had she made them think they needed to save her? That it was Jules's fault they were both in this predicament? Why couldn't either of them move beyond the same, stupid patterns of behavior? She was so—

A splash behind her interrupted her spiral, followed by a wild, retching cough. Ava swam as hard as she could toward the sound, to find Jules paddling weakly, still coughing out water. They looked like they might slip back below the surface again at any moment. She reached them just as their head went under and wrapped her arm around Jules's chest, pulling them back up. Jules coughed out an apology.

"Couldn't— Sorry, I—"

"It's okay," Ava said. "Shh, it's alright, just try to breathe."

Jules shook their head. Salt water was dripping out of their hair, down their face, into their tightly shut eyes. "I tried. I swam as far as I could, but I wasn't—I couldn't."

They coughed out a sob. It was an awful sound, lonely and wretched. Ava squeezed her arm tighter around Jules, even though it made it harder to keep them afloat.

"It's okay," Ava said.

"We're going to die out here and it's my fault," Jules wailed, their voice breaking in the middle under the salt water's assault.

Ava shook her head. "It's not."

"It is! I always do this, I try and fix things and I make them even worse—"

"Listen to me!" she shouted. "This is not your fault. It's Tricia's for sending us. And corporate's, they're the ones that cut the FINNA teams in the first place."

A moment of quiet. Jules's breathing was beginning to even out. "I guess that's true," they said shakily.

"Capitalism," said Ava.

Jules huffed a laugh. "Yep."

They were both quiet for a moment. Now that she was no longer alone, Ava felt the panic ebbing out of her. It was an odd feeling. She'd lived with fear and anxiety for so long, and fell into fits of dread and despair over the smallest things. Going to work. Making a dentist appointment. Grocery shopping. The light right after the sun went down, when she realized she'd accomplished almost nothing that day. All normal things that normal people could deal with, and she was never equal to the challenge of them. Catastrophe seemed to lurk around every corner, and she felt constantly out of control.

Now Ava was literally at sea, in an alien universe, at the whim of her shitty retail job. She had no control. Her limbs were already drifting toward exhaustion. And she was calm.

"We should conserve our energy," she said softly.

"Why?" Jules said brokenly. "What's the point?"

There was no point, and they both knew it. So Ava ignored the question. "Here, float on your back," she said, thinking of long-ago swim lessons. "Like this."

She let Jules go and shifted in the water until she was horizontal, arms and legs akimbo. The salty water buoyed her, made her feel weightless.

"What if we float away from each other?" Jules asked.

Ava turned her hand over, holding it out to them.

So they floated like that, quietly holding hands. It felt too normal for the situation. Here they were in another universe, facing death by drowning and/or hypothermia—but the touch, the calmness, felt, in some ways, more normal than the last three days, since Jules had walked out of Ava's apartment. More normal even than the month preceding it, after the shift in their relationship that Ava couldn't articulate but that she felt in her bones; her body knew it had been the end, looming. And it had been sudden and inexplicable and, like all ends, utterly implacable. The more desperately Jules had tried to fix it, the more irreparable it seemed.

But that wasn't quite it, was it? The more Jules had tried to fix things between them, the more broken *Ava* had felt. Breaking up with Jules felt like the only way she could salvage anything of herself.

Ava imagined what the two of them looked like from far above: two bright specks against the dark sea, dressed in the same sky-blue polos and khaki pants. She wondered if their bodies would ever be found; if there was life in this sea that would eat them, take nourishment from them.

"Do you think there's a universe out there where we didn't break up?" she asked Jules.

Jules was quiet a moment, then answered. "There are infinite universes."

"So there are universes where we . . . worked. Where my brain wasn't garbage."

"And I didn't run away from my problems."

Ava thought she should argue, but she was too exhausted. "Where we stayed together, had a big gay wedding, adopted kids, and then died together. In our nineties, in the same bed."

Jules snorted. They knew *The Notebook* had left an outsized impression on Ava's preteen mind. "Sure," they said.

"And just as many universes where we never met at all. Or stayed together and were completely miserable."

"Or broke up and managed to be friends." There was salt in her mouth; seawater or tears, maybe both.

"Infinite iterations," Jules said. Their voice was hardly more than a whisper, but Ava could hear everything Jules was feeling in those two words: grief, but also acceptance, and just a hint of the wonder that always animated Jules, an abiding surprise with the world. They had told her once that they'd never expected to live to be twenty-five, and they still had a hard time imagining that they'd live to be thirty. It had seemed like too much to ask for, as a Black, trans teenager of immigrant parents. Thirty years had felt like an unreasonable expectation. *So every day is like a gift,* Ava had said. It had been early in their relationship, and every night had stretched into cycles of sex and kissing and rambling postcoital conversation.

Existence isn't a gift, it's a right, Jules had replied. *But having to reclaim it every day makes life easier to appreciate, maybe.*

Ava squeezed Jules's hand, wishing she had the energy to articulate her feelings. She'd wished that she could have felt a fraction of their appreciation for existence.

"Do you hear that?" Jules said.

"Hear what?" Ava asked, but she realized that she did: a soft pinging sound from the water, like an underwater bell. Ava counted six pings before a flurry of bubbles erupted all around her and Jules.

What now? she thought, sure the two of them were about to be eaten by a whale. The previously calm water churned, buffeting them with waves. Ava lost her grip on Jules's hand and was briefly sucked under the water, only to realize that there was something sturdy underneath her hands and knees. It rose steadily up and out of the water: a giant, dark gray surface, pebbled enough that she could stand on it without slipping. As the enormous thing breached beneath her, Ava thought again of a whale, but it seemed too broad, a surface nearly the breadth of a city block, the shape of a baseball diamond. Maybe she was going to be eaten by a giant manta ray. How novel.

A few feet away, she saw Jules scramble after something. The FINNA, she realized, and she watched it bounce and roll toward the edge. Jules caught it just before it toppled off, back into the water.

"This is real, right?" Ava asked them. "I'm not hallucinating from hypothermia?"

"Maybe we both are," Jules called back. They stood on shaky legs, making their way back so the two of them could stand together. "But also, we're in a different universe, so who actually knows."

Ava looked closer as the pebbled skin of whatever they

were standing on and found rivets in it. "I think it's a ship."

"Then what's that?" Jules asked. They raised a trembling finger, and Ava followed it. They were pointing at a mound in the center of the—the hull, Ava thought, the word coming to her from the brief two months when she had entertained fantasies about joining the navy, which she'd indulged by binging sailor movies.

A hatch atop the mound in the hull suddenly sprang open with a hiss of air. A figure climbed halfway out of it; an older woman in a high-collared coat, crimson with sky-blue piping.

"Ahoy!" Jules called to her. Then, to Ava: "That's what people say on boats, right?"

Ava was looking closer at the woman who had just climbed out onto the hull. She yanked open the waterlogged purse she'd found in the deadly garden Liten-Värld, miraculously still over her shoulder, and pulled out the pocketbook, flipping it open to look at the driver's license.

"Ahoy yourselves!" Ursula Nouri called. Or at least, this universe's approximation of her. "You seem like you could use a lift!"

CHAPTER SIX

Ava had never been on a submarine before. Her initial assessment: maybe she should look back into being a naval seaman. The hallways were low-ceilinged but wide, with strips of light glowing blue and green and red, jewel-bright and cheerful. Brass dials and instruments littered most of surfaces, and layers of graffiti crowded any empty space. It was certainly better than the fluorescent lights and smooth jazz covers of pop songs that were hallmarks of working retail.

"Welcome aboard the *L. V. Anahita,* merchant class vessel," the woman said. "I'm Captain Nouresh."

She looked them over and they did the same. Captain Nouresh had a thick braid of white hair that hung down one shoulder, and wore black high-waisted pants and a white linen shirt underneath her coat. She looked stunningly similar to the old woman Ava had seen in the photo on the young woman's phone, though her hair was longer, her face paler, and she had a few extra scars.

"You're travelers then?" Nouresh asked. "Through the marejii?" At Ava's blank stare, she amended, "Sorry, what do you call them? The hallways between worlds."

"Maskhål," Ava answered.

"Wormholes," Jules corrected. "Our stupid boss at LitenVärld calls them maskhål, because they're a Swedish corporation."

Nouresh looked at them blankly. "I thought I could still speak your language, but maybe I was wrong."

"Wait, how *can* you speak our language?" Ava said, wringing out her hair.

"I'm a traveler myself," Nouresh said, bowing with an ironic flourish. "I spent my youth navigating the marejii. I stayed for some months in a city where they spoke your language. It was called Annapolis."

Jules and Ava shared a look. "I have no idea where that is."

"Minnesota?" Ava guessed.

"I think that's Minneapolis." Jules looked back at the captain. "Sorry, we haven't traveled much."

"No? It's a beautiful city of bricks, at the crossroads of a river and the sea. I was happy there for a while."

Jules and Ava said that it sounded very nice, wherever it was. (Maine? Maryland? They'd have to check the LitenVärld directory.) Then Ava gave a performative shiver and asked, "Is there a place we can get some dry clothes?"

"I'll take you to the market," Nouresh said. "Follow me."

They followed the older woman through a series of halls, all of them similarly low-ceilinged, and lit with the same emerald lights that Jules eventually pointed out looked alive. "They are," Nouresh said. "Tiny creatures that give off light."

"Bioluminescent plankton!" Jules said. "That's so cool!"

Nouresh seemed bemused by their outburst, and Ava explained, "They said the same thing about a chair that almost ate them."

"Oh, the Soft Snare? In Universe 241?"

Captain Nouresh, it seemed, had compiled a taxonomy of the universes she had traveled to in her youth, in service to something called the Cooperative of Nations. She'd taken detailed descriptions, notes on languages, flora and fauna, dominant species and their social structures. Ava could see Jules's eyes growing wide as she told them of the places and things that she had seen.

Wanderlust. Ava had never really had it. Jules always had. They'd always felt stuck, both at LitenVärld and in their hometown, where they had returned after dropping out of college. Ava was aware of this large portion of Jules's life that they didn't discuss—what had happened at their school, why they had dropped out, why they had come back home afterward—but never asked about it, even during that first, dizzying flush of falling in love. Ava had always skirted it; she'd thought that she was giving Jules room and space to bring it up on their own schedule, but they never had. And she'd assumed that now they never would, but maybe that could change.

"How many worlds did you come through?" Captain Nouresh asked.

"Three?" Ava said. "It's hard to tell. I couldn't spot all of the seams."

"Not bad, for a first trip. What made you leave your world? And what are you using to navigate?"

Jules looked at Ava. "We were actually—"

"Using this old piece of shit," Ava interrupted, pulling the FINNA out of Jules's grasp. "Didn't hold up to the water, though."

Captain Nouresh cooed at the FINNA like it was a small, injured animal. "Oh, look at this. Haven't seen one of these since I was your age."

She pressed one of its buttons and it beeped at her, the sound warbly and sad. "Shouldn't be too hard to fix. These things were designed to take a beating."

Ava hadn't realized how deeply she was afraid of not being able to get home until Nouresh said that. A tight knot of muscles loosened in the center of her back, and she was able to breathe.

"It'll take me some time," the captain said. "In the

meantime, though, I'm sure you'll be able to occupy yourself."

She stuck the FINNA in the deep pocket of her coat, and wrenched open a door. The noise hit Ava first, a cheerful hubbub of voices, music, bodies, and business. She shared a quick look with Jules and felt a pulse of excitement pass between the two of them. She followed Jules through the hatch and into a wild, chaotic bazaar.

Vendors stood in front of a labyrinth of stalls. The ceiling here was higher, and tent walls stretched up toward it, rippling with movement as large, leaf-shaped fans circulated the air in the room.

The market—which stretched the resemblance to the LitenVärld she knew—didn't take cash, only trade. Jules, veteran of many church basement rummage sales, found a table with piles of clothing to trade in their seawater-soaked uniform. They reappeared in what looked like sailor's garb: a cotton shirt, loose pants, and a coat, though they had to give up the steel-toed sneakers they'd bought at Kmart in order to work in stocking and assembly. They seemed happier to be barefoot.

"Nice," Ava said, catching sight of them after they haggled. "You fit right in."

Ava ended up trading in the bottle of Ursula's perfume along with her uniform for a tunic, skirt, and a warm knitted shawl. She felt guilty, but also figured that Ursula wouldn't miss the bottle, and her granddaughter wouldn't realize it was gone.

"Thanks," Jules said. "You look . . . comfortable."

"Wow," Ava said drily. "Great." She'd picked out clothing as close to pajamas as she could find, and probably didn't look anywhere near as cool as Jules.

"In a good way!" Jules said, holding up their hands. "It's been a while since I've seen you look anything besides . . ."

Ava could fill in the blank. *Miserable. Angry. Depressed.* Fair enough.

"Let's get some food," she said, and Jules nodded.

They followed their noses toward the center of the market, and found a plethora of food stalls. The food stalls, weirdly, shared names with the chains and franchises that Ava found herself eating at too often in their shitty suburb. The Olive Grove had mounds of freshly baked pita bread and hummus. Dumpling Express was half-obscured by clouds of fragrant steam, serving little bundles wrapped tightly in leaves. El Buckarito, the worst Tex-Mex chain to have ever given Ava food poisoning, offered skewers of grilled meat and vegetables, liberally coated with spices.

Jules tapped on Ava's shoulder, and she turned to find them pointing at a sign that said Pasta and Friends, staffed by a single old man hand-rolling noodles.

"Think they take gift cards?" Jules asked.

"Who said I was going to share?" Ava asked. She relished Jules's look of utter betrayal before handing them one.

The noodles were delicious, and Captain Nouresh graciously bought them a round of sweet, ginger-flavored wine to drink with their meal. Jules eventually got distracted by a group of kids kicking a ball around—they always said that soccer was a language that transcended all borders, and apparently that held true across the multiverse—and Captain Nouresh started tinkering with the waterlogged FINNA, pulling out a set of tools from a pouch on her belt.

"You should tell her," Jules whispered, right before they went off with the kids. "Why we're here."

Ava had actually managed to forget, for a while, that they were on a mission from their lords and masters at LitenVärld. She resented the reminder; it was nice to blame LitenVärld for making them face murderous clones and carnivorous chairs, but she didn't want to credit her corporate overlords for sending her here, the first new world that actually seemed cool.

"Do you often get travelers like us?" Ava asked Captain Nouresh. "Coming through wormholes?"

The captain poked confidently and curiously through the guts of the FINNA as she spoke. She sketched out the world of the *Anahita,* one of a class of merchant ships that moved between underwater city-states, migratory nations that traversed the ocean's surface, and the nomadic townships that hung at the edges of both.

"I wonder if our universe is some kind of hub for others, if we have more marejii. Or maybe it's just that our ships know to look for travelers."

Captain Nouresh pulled a magnifying eyepiece out of her pocket, peering closer at the circuitry in the FINNA. "It seemed like your world was so scared of strangers and strangeness. It gets covered up, renamed, cut up until it fits into a familiar skin. Like this." She gestured at the guts of the FINNA, now spread out across their table. Ava was struck by how different some of the components were; there were bits of plastic, a circuit board, and the hex bolts that were a hallmark of all LitenVärld design. But other components were utterly alien: something that looked like neon-orange moss, crystals that glowed a dusky pink, bright brass gears, a glass vial that contained a swirling, crimson gas. "I can see the work of three different worlds in here, maybe four. But all they want you to see is this."

She tapped the white LitenVärld logo on the gray plastic cover: the letters L and V in a cutesy, corporate font, and nestled between them, a sphere chopped into meridians and parallels. Ava thought about the training video, and the specs of the FINNA on the instructions booklet: *Property of LitenVärld Inc., LLC.*

Now that she thought of it, that same phrase had been printed onto the sky-blue polo that was her uniform, just below the tags. A reminder and a warning. Jules often called their job soul-killing, raged that retail was designed to wear down wage workers into hapless drones, too scared of poverty to rise up in revolution. *It's just a job,* she'd always said. *No better or worse than any other job.*

That's exactly the problem, Jules would groan.

Much as "Ugh, capitalism" was a running joke between them, their system was too big to do anything *but* joke about it. It's not like they had a plethora of options waiting for them out there.

But now there were options. Doorways into other worlds and other possibilities opened all the time, apparently. LitenVärld liked its worlds small, contained in their claustrophobic cubes, and under their control. No wonder they had gotten rid of the FINNA division. Ava wondered what they had found out there; what they'd brought back, what ideas they'd been infected with. Maybe some teams had chosen not to come back at all.

"Ah," said Captain Nouresh, who'd continued to work while Ava was lost in thought. She set down her tools, wound the wires back into the FINNA's shell, and flicked the switch again. There was a brief pop, and Ava flinched back, worried it would explode. But beyond a puff of briny-smelling vapor, the FINNA seemed fine. The bubble lit up purple again, and the console—despite some moisture under the glass screen—flashed and came back on. There was no arrow, though; instead, a bull's-eye blinked.

"That's amazing," Ava said, taking it back from Nouresh.

Nouresh smiled wryly and put her tools away. "I've got a way with old and useless things, being one myself."

Ava looked up at the captain. "You don't seem useless to me."

In fact, she was one of the most formidable women she'd ever met. Aside from Jules's aunt, who Jules had lived with briefly, and who wasn't formidable as much as she was actively horrible.

Nouresh shrugged. "I should have passed control of the *Anahita* to my first mate years ago. She's still young, but plenty capable."

"What would you do instead?" Ava asked. She wasn't sure how she was going to convince Nouresh to come with them. More intel couldn't hurt.

But Nouresh gave her a thin, brittle smile. "That's the question, isn't it? All the captains I admired retired to a seafloor grave." Her smile shifted, became stronger, realer. "I would have happily gone down with my ship, but that would have meant losing a battle, and I was never very good at that. So here we are, the *Anahita* and I."

After watching her put away her tools, Ava offered tentatively, "You could travel again? If you retired?"

"I could," Nouresh agreed, though she didn't sound excited by it.

"But you don't want to," said Ava.

Nouresh shrugged. "Getting lost for lack of a better option loses its appeal after a while. I've already got too much free time for comfort. How else do you think I was able to wine and dine you and your ..." She looked at Jules for a moment, then back to Ava. "Partner?"

Ava swallowed thickly. "Not anymore," she said. It was the first time she'd actually said it aloud to anyone. She'd texted her friends, emailed her brother, but hadn't actually said it aloud until now. Three days, the words had been kept in her throat.

"Ah," Nouresh said delicately.

"I think we could be friends, though?" Ava said. Now that she'd started to speak, she couldn't seem to stop. "Like, we never really got to that stage. We went straight from coworkers to crush to codependent dating. Traveling with them has almost been easier, despite all the stuff that's been trying to kill us." Ava watched Jules showing off their soccer skills, kicking the ball up, catching it on their chest where it seemed to hang, defying gravity for a moment, before dropping it onto the ground again. The kids fell momentarily silent in amazement, then started yelling in excitement as they tried to get the ball back from Jules, and then each other. A couple of kids started fiercely arguing, and Jules held up their hands, trying to circumvent a fight.

"There are beautiful worlds out there, you know," Captain Nouresh said. "You might want to take the long way back, once you find whatever it is you're looking for. It might help you find your footing with each other."

Ava looked from the bull's-eye to Nouresh, who met her gaze calmly. She really did look a lot like the young woman at the customer service counter. Ava set the FINNA down. "Can I ask you something? Do you have a family?"

Nouresh's face changed, falling a little. She looked older. "Not anymore," she said.

"I'm sorry," Ava said. Sorry for bringing it up, sorry for dragging that unnamed hurt out of the past. *Appropriate replacement,* she thought. What an awful way of thinking about it. Was that why the FINNA had led them to Nouresh? Some algorithm had matched her grief to the hole Ursula would leave in their world?

"It's an old sadness," Nouresh said. "Doesn't heal, but you get used to bearing it."

Ava nodded, thinking again of Ursula's granddaughter.

Ava had never been particularly close to her own grandparents, not like the girl—whose name she didn't even know, she realized. All Ava could think of was the way the young woman had stared at the selfie, the way her worry seemed to diminish her in size and age, make her a child again.

The captain's eyes suddenly cut away from Ava, narrowing as something else caught her attention. Ava turned to look as well, at Jules. They had managed to distract the kids with a story about their recent misadventures in the so-called hive. The kids watched, entranced as Jules acted it out with their whole body. They'd drawn a sizable crowd, some of whom surely couldn't understand the words Jules spoke. But Jules had always been a dynamic storyteller, and the past few hours had given them even more fodder.

"And then, they look at each other and say, let's take them to *Mother*. Mother wants to meet you. Mother wants you to answer some questions. And we're like—" Jules made a comically fearful face, but nobody seemed to laugh. Instead, they all looked nervous.

There was a fierce grip on her arm, and Ava turned back to find Captain Nouresh looking at her intently.

"You came here through a hive?"

Disquiet squirmed in Ava's chest. "That's what they called it."

Nouresh cursed under her breath, then squeezed Ava's arm in a tighter grip. "Answer me truthfully. Did they see you come through the marejii?"

Ava hesitated, suddenly afraid—not just of the weird LitenVärld murder clones, but selfishly, of angering the woman in front of her. "Yes? I mean, I don't know. We were running from them, they chased us to a pit, and the maskhål was below us, so Jules threw us both into it."

Nouresh stood, yanking Ava to her feet as well. She pulled her along toward Jules, and snapped, "You! With me!"

Jules flinched at the shout, but then leapt to their feet, looking to Ava for explanation. Before she could offer it, Captain Nouresh—and Ava realized that she was definitely looking at the *captain* now, a woman who had run an enormous ship for years, with such efficiency that she'd made herself redundant—pulled Ava along through the market. Jules darted along behind them.

CHAPTER SEVEN

"What happened? What's going on?" Jules asked, trying to keep up with Nouresh's ruthless pace.

"The hive," Ava said breathlessly. "I don't know, she just—"

"Quiet!" Nouresh snapped. She'd led them out of the labyrinthine market, over to one of the round, curved walls, lit with those strips of glowing plankton. She dashed along it, finally letting go of Ava in her haste. Ava chased after her.

Captain Nouresh reached a metal cabinet set into the wall that was painted a bright red, the same color as the captain's jacket, unlike the calm, muted colors the *Anahita* had shown them so far. There was writing above it, but of course Ava couldn't read it. It reminded her of the fancy Arabic calligraphy she'd seen at an exhibit at the Art Institute.

"The hives swarm when they're threatened. They've followed travelers through the marejii before," Captain Nouresh said as she flung open the cabinet doors. There were complicated brass instruments in it, and a black square of glass. A phone? Nouresh twisted the instruments in a complicated pattern, then yanked a cylinder toward her face.

With a flash of light across the black glass panel, Ava realized that it was actually a steampunk video chat. The face on the screen wore a jacket nearly identical to the captain's, and was older than Ava but younger than Nouresh. Nouresh spat orders in another language, but the woman interrupted her, holding a hand up, as if in reassurance.

An alarm blared, an incessant clanging that set everyone in the market bustling. Ava's heart was hammering in her chest, but the merchants calmly began to fold up their tents and stow their wares. The group of children Jules had been playing with ran past, but even their faces didn't betray much fear.

When Ava looked back at Captain Nouresh, she was still exchanging words with the woman on the screen. *Her second-in-command?* Ava wondered. The woman curled her hand into a loose fist and touched her knuckles to her chin, with a short bow. Captain Nouresh returned the odd salute, and the screen flickered off. Nouresh took a deep breath, then slammed the metal doors of the cabinet shut.

"You two!" she barked. "Follow me."

Ava shot Jules a look, and they shrugged at each other

before jogging to catch up with Nouresh, who moved calmly and quickly through the narrow passageways of the *Anahita*. "The two of you were searching for someone, correct? That's why you were sent?"

Jules shot Ava a worried look. "Yeah," they said. "How did you know?"

"Your toy there," she said, and Ava realized she meant the FINNA. "I've seen them before. The people carrying them were always traveling to bring someone back to their original world."

"Yeah," Ava said. "Yeah, we were sent to find someone."

"It would be a good time to find another marejii and continue your search," Nouresh said. "The hive followed you here. The crew spotted them right before you told me."

"That was the alarm?" Jules asked. They seemed calm. Why did they seem so calm about this?

"Yes. The bridge crew have it under control. My first mate . . ." Nouresh clenched her jaw. "It shouldn't be a problem for her, but in case this battle doesn't go the way we think it will, you should leave now."

Jules raised their eyebrows at Ava, as if to say, *That's your cue.* Ava took a deep breath, trying to work around the panic that was pressing against her skull, and said, "We found who we were looking for. It's you."

The captain stopped in her tracks, looking over her shoulder at the two of them. "What did you say?"

"A version of you, anyway," Ava corrected. She fumbled out the pocketbook in Ursula's purse, holding up the driver's license. Nouresh took it gingerly. "This is who we were sent to find, but she . . ."

"Got eaten. We think," Jules said.

"I always knew other versions of me existed," Nouresh said, staring at the license. "It's strange to be confronted with evidence." She looked at Ava. "If she's dead, why did you keep looking?"

Ava lifted the flap on the pocketbook that held the driver's license. On the other side was the photo of Ursula and her emo-phase granddaughter. There weren't any other photos in the pocketbook—no children, no other family members, no pets. This had been the most important person in Ursula's life, the only one whose picture was worthy of being kept on her at all times.

"Her granddaughter. She's older now, and I only met her for a minute," Ava said. "But she seemed nice. Scared. And alone."

"The FINNA looks for the most, uh, appropriate replacement if the original person is gone. It decided that meant you," added Jules.

"Did it now," Captain Nouresh said softly. She swallowed, then tossed the pocketbook back to Ava. "Doesn't matter. A captain never abandons her ship during a battle."

Ava fumbled to catch the pocketbook, and by the time she'd shoved it back into the purse, Nouresh had resumed walking at her fast clip. Ava hurried to keep pace.

Nouresh stopped in front of a door, painted that same bloody red. This one had a complicated brass locking mechanism. She took a breath, leaned into something that looked like a shallow satellite dish, and said softly, "Uzmala Nouresh."

There was a soft, metallic tinkling sound, and then a clank, components moving and shifting until the door swung inward.

"This place is so cool," Jules whispered.

"Agreed," Ava replied.

The two of them followed Captain Nouresh into a circular room about the size of Ava's bedroom. It was dominated by a large table with a high lip around the edge, like an enormous ashtray. Its top was covered with a thick layer of sand. After shutting the door behind them, Nouresh shouldered Ava and Jules aside to stand beside the table. She spoke, again in that soft voice of command, then plunged her hands beneath the surface, sending ripples through the sand as if it were water. A large bubble bulged out from the center. It grew eyes, claws, and a mouth pulled from a thousand insects that had devoured

Ava in a thousand nightmares. (She had extremely specific phobias, she could admit.) "That's the mother?" Jules asked, quicker on the uptake than Ava.

"Oh, *god*!" Ava said. That eldritch nightmare had lived in the pit below the clone LitenVärld. "That's the thing that almost *ate* us?"

The sand floated up above the table, joined by numerous smaller blobs that slowly formed into small, human shapes, so many of them that they formed a cloud of satellites, blurring as they swam in darting orbits. The Marks and Danas of the hive, Ava assumed.

Nouresh smiled grimly. "Hello, you old bitch. Thought you'd find a new hive, did you?"

"We're gonna fight that?" Jules asked excitedly. Ava, feeling sick with fear, glared at them.

"My crew is going to fight that. It's time to see if my first mate can actually—"

As she spoke, another bubble floated up from the sand, transforming into a manta-shaped vessel slightly larger than the mother. It twisted, turning in the air, and all three of them felt a tug of gravity as the ship shifted.

"Good," Nouresh said. "Get them gunside. Now, let's see if—"

There was a muted *clap-clap, clap-clap, clap-clap* somewhere in the bowels of the ship. The miniature above the table shot off tiny darts that carved through the air toward the mother and her swarm. Torpedos, Ava assumed. The small humans that swam next to the mother broke away, swimming to intercept them. They exploded in showers of sand that fell gently back onto the table. Others made it through the swarm and exploded on the mother itself, leaving hollow craters in her sides. The sand-mother opened her mouth wide, but the terrifying screech came from all around them, leaking through the metal walls. Ava clapped her hands over her ears and shrank away from the table. The muscles in her legs felt hot and heavy, barely able to keep her upright.

Ava took strength from looking at Captain Nouresh. The intent look hadn't left her face, but she was smiling now. "Good opening gambit, Mirya. What next?"

As if in answer, the *Anahita* released its own swarm of tiny, darting objects.

"Minnows," Nouresh said contemplatively. "Interesting play."

"Are they like drones?" Jules asked, leaning in. Sections of the mother's swarm broke off to chase the minnows, which flew gracefully but in unpredictable, zigzagging patterns. Nouresh glanced over her shoulder, distracted for a moment.

"I don't know 'drones,'" Nouresh said distractedly. "We send them out to collect information, samples. I've never thought to use them as a distraction. Mirya's good."

The praise sounded forced. "Well, she learned from you, right?" Jules said.

"She did," Nouresh admitted. More than half the swarm had abandoned the mother to chase after the minnows. The *Anahita* shot off another series of torpedoes, which sank into the mother's unprotected flank. The mother roared again, shaking the walls, reverberating through Ava's bones.

"Not bad," Nouresh said. She was smiling now. "Are you going to finish her off?"

Before she'd finished speaking, an even larger missile shot off toward the mother, aiming right for her open maw. There was a half second of quiet, and then an enormous, muffled *thump*. The mother exploded, spraying grit into all of their faces.

"Eugh," Ava said, spitting out grains. They were tasteless, but she couldn't help but think of them as part of the mother. She froze as an eerie chorus of wails cut through the room, echoing off the walls.

"Her children," Nouresh said. "I would have spent a few more missiles killing them off. They're cunning little bastards, and they've got a bad tendency to sneak aboard ships. Should be impossible, but they always find a way." She lifted her hands out of the semi-liquid sand, and the simulacra of the swarm and the *Anahita* fell back onto the table.

"Did we win?" Jules asked. "That was the battle?"

Nouresh nodded, wiping her hands off. "They used to be longer and bloodier, back when I was a fresh recruit. But we've evolved our tactics and they haven't. They'll keep doing the same thing until they go extinct." She went over to a cabinet on the wall, similar to the one in the market. Nouresh opened the doors, twisting instruments until the black screen lit up again. The first mate's face appeared; she looked sweaty, nervous and excited. She saluted, stumbling over the greeting—maybe she hadn't expected to face the captain so soon after the battle. Captain Nouresh held up a hand to cut her off. "Mirya."

Captain Nouresh spoke, her tone calm and professional, and more than a little proud.

If anything, the first mate looked even more nervous. She replied with confusion and concern. Nouresh's smile grew, and her voice became cheerful. There was a hissed whisper behind Mirya, which she hushed. "Uzmala?" she said. The captain's first name, Ava remembered. Mirya asked a question. Nouresh gave no answer, just a salute. Then she cut the connection and closed the cabinet doors.

"What did you tell her?" Ava asked.

"I congratulated her on her overdue promotion to captain, and told her where to find the letter of commission.

I wrote it months ago, but haven't been able to give up the ship." Captain Nouresh touched the wall affectionately, like an old friend or a family member. She patted it a couple of times, then said, "I'm ready for my next adventure. It's been too long since I've walked through a marejii."

Ava felt an enormous weight lift off her chest. She listened with half an ear as Jules excitedly told Nouresh about their own world, all the amazing places in it besides Annapolis—though of course Nouresh could go back there, if she wanted, but she should know about some other options. Jules's secondhand wanderlust was palpable, and contagious, judging by Nouresh's face.

All Ava could think was that they were going *home*. She liked the *Anahita,* and maybe if she'd chosen this she would have been able to enjoy the traveling, like Jules obviously was. But she hadn't signed up for this, and she was ready to be back in her own universe, back in her apartment, with her books, and her bed, and hours of sitcoms cued up on her laptop.

Still, she cleared her throat to get Nouresh and Jules's attention and said, "Maybe we can say we lost the FINNA. Say it got eaten by a chair or something."

Nouresh smiled at the scheming look on Jules's face. "Some of my information is out of date, but I'd be happy to give you some pointers on traveling through the marejii."

Jules turned their grin to Ava. "Pretty sure you can get fired for stealing from the job."

Ava shrugged. Going home was good, but the thought of going back to LitenVärld was exhausting. Moreover, it was making her realize how draining her time there was; how much energy that shit job stole from her every day. "It's not like they're using it," she replied. "And we can keep them from sending other workers to get eaten by chairs."

"Worker solidarity, nice," Jules said. They held their fist out, and Ava bumped it. As they shared a smile, Ava noticed that it didn't hurt. For the first time in a long time, the sight of Jules's grin didn't press against something exquisitely painful inside her, or ignite a toxic well. Jules smiled because they were happy, and Ava smiled back, because it was good to see Jules happy. Simple as that.

They turned the corner and walked into a nightmare.

CHAPTER EIGHT

One of the Danas stood in front of them, dripping with seawater and black smears of grease. Her sky-blue polo clung to her ribcage, giving her a sunken, cadaverous look.

Ava's fear didn't have a chance to drag her down or cloud her mind. Her senses sharpened until she could see the individual lines of grease trickling down the Dana's arm, hear the water drip off her clothes and hair and hit the floor. The Dana's lips pulled back from her teeth, which looked like they'd gotten sharper. In the store, the Danas all had nice French manicures, but now there was muck embedded underneath the nails and in the beds.

"Where is my mother, shoppers?" she asked.

Nouresh shoved Ava back toward Jules, yanking a long, curved sword out of a sheath at her belt. She gave a shout and rushed at the Dana, who dodged away from her and hissed.

Nouresh feinted with the sword, drove the Dana up against the wall, and then thrust a dagger into her chest. It barely seemed to faze the Dana, who screeched in

Nouresh's face and swiped at her with her claws. Nouresh danced back, graceful as a cat.

"Run!" she shouted at Jules and Ava. She took another swing at the Dana with her dagger, catching her in the hand and taking off several of her fingers. The Dana shrieked and cradled her hand, which bled a dark, viscous ooze from the stumps. There were a dozen answering screeches from further down the hallway.

Ava's brain, which had done such a great job of observing, remembered that it was supposed to be *running like hell* and also *scared shitless*. There was a door ahead of them, and Ava's focus narrowed to it, to the small oblong opening and the thick door that stood ajar in front of it.

She started to shut the doorway behind her, only to realize that she was alone. Ava yanked the door back—no easy feat, the thing weighed significantly more than she did—and looked back down the hallway. Jules was a few dozen steps behind her, carrying Nouresh in their arms.

Nouresh, who was covered in blood, and looked half-conscious.

"Help us!" Jules yelled, but again, Ava's feet were already carrying her toward them. She and Jules muscled Nouresh through the narrow hatchway, tripping over the tall lip, and slammed the door shut on the echoing shrieks of the Marks and Danas. There was a wheel in the center that Jules quickly spun, just as a series of thuds hit the door.

"Lock it!" Ava cried, taking Nouresh's weight and laying her on the floor.

"How?" Jules was straining with the wheel, muscles in their forearms standing out like cords. Ava could tell it was all Jules could do to hold the door against them, there was no chance of twisting it shut and locked. An unholy wailing rose up, and the sounds of scratching, muffled by the thick walls.

Nouresh moaned, a pained, pitiful sound. "What happened to her?" Ava demanded.

"She put one down, but another snuck up behind her," Jules said through clenched teeth. "Started tearing into her before I knocked it away. She lopped off its head but fainted after that."

Ava, hands shaking, knocked the sword out of Nouresh's slack grip and grasped her wrist, trying to find a pulse. It was there, but sluggish. Ava nudged open her coat: there were wide, gaping tears across the front of Nouresh's shirt, and the fabric was sodden with blood, as red as the captain's coat.

"Shit," Ava said, trying and failing to remember the mandatory first aid classes she'd sat through six months before. They'd just been another series of instructional videos, which were apparently LitenVärld's answer to everything. She yanked off her own shawl and tied it around the wounds. Pressure, right? To stop bleeding? It would have to do for now.

"Okay, we have to get out of here," Ava said, fumbling for the FINNA. "Fuck this fucking place and all the fucking monsters and this fucking job—!"

She finally got the stupid thing out of Ursula's giant granny purse right as the wheel slid underneath Jules' hands. With a shout of effort, they stopped its movement. "I can't hold it for long!" they shouted. "Get my belt off!"

Ava looked back at them. "What?"

"Use my belt to tie the hatch closed. It'll stop them for a while!"

Ava stumbled over, yanked Jules's shirt up, and managed to pull their belt through the loops. She slid it through the rim of the wheel, looped it around a metal handhold, and then cinched the whole thing shut. She could feel minute shudders coming through the door as the Danas and Marks slammed against it. It was, what, four inches of solid metal? Christ.

Finally, it was done. Jules relaxed minutely; their knuckles, pale with strain, flushed as blood flowed back into them. Then the wheel gave a short, aborted turn. The leather belt creaked ominously against the sudden strain, and the buckle started to bend.

"Fuck!" Jules shouted, and grabbed hold of it again. "Get the FINNA!"

Ava scrabbled for it again, finally getting the unwieldy thing into her hands. "Home, home, how do I make it take us home?"

"This is why you should read the instructions!"

"Really, Jules?!" Ava screamed. "Because I might need to escape from a swarm of cannibal drones?"

Jules took a precious second to pull the instructional booklet out of their back pocket and throw it at Ava. She snatched it out of the air and opened it. The diagrams swam before her eyes like an alien script. "How can anyone make any sense of this shit?" she hissed.

Jules said, "Check page twelve, that's where I found the other instructions."

Ava flipped to page twelve and found the diagrams, right where Jules said they were: a happy cartoon person flipping the dial on the side from the compass to a house. Intuitive design. A house for home. Sure. She turned the dial on the side of the FINNA; there was a musical beep, and a new blue arrow popped up on the console, directing them down through another hallway. "Okay, I think I got it. Let's get the hell out of here."

She began the process of hauling Nouresh up, trying not to think the word *deadweight*. "Can you help me with her?"

"I don't think I should," Jules said. Their voice was strained, but curiously calm. Ava looked back over her shoulder. Jules's muscles were quivering under their dark skin, shaking with the effort of holding the wheel.

"You go," they said. "I'll stay and hold them back as long as I can."

It was as if Jules had said it in French, which Ava had never been able to understand. The words made no sense, not separately nor strung together. Stay where? Hold who?

"Shut up and stop being stupid," Ava blurted. Not her finest or most mature comeback.

"You stop being stupid!" Jules replied. At least they were on the same wavelength.

"What the hell are you even saying?" Ava shouted.

"It's bad enough that they followed us into this world!" Jules shouted back. "Can you imagine what would happen if we led them back to ours?"

Would they do that? The mother was dead, but what if one of the Marks or Danas was like, a hive queen-in-waiting? Was that possible? The only person who could tell them was unconscious and possibly bleeding out in Ava's arms.

"Okay, but—" Ava started to say, though she had no idea what she was going to follow it with.

"I don't have to hold them off forever," Jules said. "The

crew will come eventually. They can hear the alarm. Besides, even if they get through"—they nodded at Ava's foot, where the curved blade of Captain Nouresh's sword lay in a puddle of blood—"I can hold them back. They can only come through this door one at a time."

"That sounds like suicide," Ava pleaded.

"Would you just trust me this fucking once?" Jules screamed. "I promise that this is not a noble sacrifice! I can do this, so give me the damn sword!"

She wondered desperately if Jules even knew how to use it, or if this was just bluster to get Ava to leave.

But on the heels of that came another thought: could she, just this once, trust Jules to know what they were capable of?

Ava bent down and, grunting with effort, hauled Nouresh's weight up over her shoulder. Then she kicked the sword over to Jules, so that they could reach down and grab it. Ava stared at them for a second. "You weren't planning on coming back, were you?" she asked, needing to confirm it.

Jules shook their head. "Didn't imagine it would be because I was holding back a swarm of violent sales associates, though."

Her eyes started burning, and her face flushed. Ava felt a wave of impatience with herself. She had already promised that she was done crying over Jules, and her hands were too covered in blood to even wipe the tears starting to scald her cheeks. This was truly not the time.

"It's okay," Jules said. They looked . . . not calm, exactly, but not scared. They looked, as they had for most of their trip, thrilled that they weren't getting misgendered while answering customers' stupid questions about how much weight a towel rod could *really* hold. "This is what I want. I'm not running from something, I'm choosing it."

Ava tried desperately to think of some final, parting words. There was so much left unsaid, but all the words were tangling themselves up in her head.

The door rattled under Jules's weight, and the smile on their face turned into a snarl. "Go!" they screamed, and Ava went, forcing herself not to look back again. Not when she heard the door slam open and the voices of the Marks and Danas come in clearly. Not even when she heard Jules's answering scream of defiance, and the sound of a sword whistling through the air.

She couldn't look back. If she didn't look back, she didn't have to know whether she was leaving Jules to their death.

The FINNA directed her through a labyrinth of passages, all of them stained yellow with what she realized were the emergency lights. First Mate Mirya apparently had more to mop up than they'd realized, because the sounds of fighting echoed down other corridors. The

FINNA, either by luck or according to some weird twist of its programming, led them only through empty corridors, dodging other battles, the *Anahita*'s crew, and the Marks and Danas they fought. Eventually, the FINNA beeped again, more urgently than it had before. Ava shifted Nouresh's weight, grimacing at the tacky feeling of blood that had soaked into her tunic, and ran faster.

She almost didn't recognize the maskhål when she saw it. This one pulsed with a sickening, reddish light, unlike any she'd seen before. The place where the worlds were stitched together wasn't a line, but stretched out, creating a tunnel made of twitching, juddering skin. But at the other end, she recognized a familiar sight: the Nihilistic Bachelor Cube.

Even as she looked, the familiar interior receded, grew more distant.

The maskhål collapsed after a couple of hours, she remembered. She thought again of the animation in that god-awful video they'd watched in the break room: the doorway between universes stretching like a piece of Silly Putty until it snapped and collapsed back on itself.

How long did she have?

"Fuck it," she said, and sprinted.

Running through the maskhål as it collapsed was like walking quickly through the showrooms at her Liten-Värld, the disorienting effect of seeing wildly different rooms stacked next to each other. The walls of the maskhål reflected and refracted images of other universes, all of them focused on her: a thousand different versions of herself, some nightmarish, some wildly surreal, others utterly mundane. All of these Avas seemed to notice something strange, looking up from whatever they were doing and staring toward Ava as she stared at them. It was dizzying, to look into these mirrors come to life. She was drawn to a set of universes that seemed perilously close to the one she was in right now: dozens and dozens of Avas trying to make their way down the tunnel of a collapsing wormhole. Some of those Avas were alone, sprinting through unburdened. In others, Captain Nouresh walked beside her, uninjured. There were more than a few where she carried Jules's bloody, lifeless body.

In some of those mirrors, she watched the tunnel tearing apart at the seams, exposing a void that writhed out of its cracks, crumbling the maskhål even faster. In others, the Avas seemed to grow desperate, distracted by the reflections that surrounded them. They took a wrong step off the path and winked out of existence. They staggered under the leaden weight of the people they carried, and finally, in desperation, dropped them. One after another, the Avas around her met their ends; some bloodless and calm, sitting down and accepting their fate, others fighting and clawing as their existence disintegrated. She didn't see a single one ahead of her, reaching the end of the tunnel and the stupid Nihilistic Bachelor Cube where this whole damn thing began. A thousand versions of herself assured her that it was hopeless.

It was a familiar refrain, one that Ava already knew how to ignore.

Ava dragged her eyes away from her reflections and focused again on the tunnel, just in time to realize that she was about to wander off the path and into the void that surrounded it. She staggered, nearly tripped, nearly dropped Nouresh, but managed to right herself. She forced the end of the tunnel to fill her vision, and pumped her weak legs even faster. It was like a nightmare; working so hard and seeming to move hardly at all.

She didn't realize it until later, but it never occurred to her to drop Captain Nouresh. That stubbornness finally was useful for something.

The other end of the maskhål loomed suddenly in front of her, her own world rearing up like a startled horse. She shoved herself and Nouresh over the threshold, into the world she knew as the wormhole snapped shut behind her.

Maybe there was a word for the way time slowed as she and Nouresh fell from the entrance of the maskhål and onto the futon in the Nihilist Bachelor Cube. Maybe it was a specific phenomenon that had been studied by physicists or LitenVärld's FINNA division. Maybe Tricia had an instructional video about it. *Spooky Action in the Workplace: Side Effects of Collapsing Wormholes and You.* Or maybe it was just the first of many PTSD symptoms that Ava could look forward to.

Whatever it was, Ava felt curiously detached as she observed the chaotic swirl of bodies around her. Tricia, Ursula Nouri's granddaughter, and half a dozen coworkers crowded around her and Nouresh. The young woman grasped Nouresh's pale, bloodstained hand in her own. Tricia yelled for someone to call for an ambulance. All of their voices were muted, as if coming from far away. Ava wondered if she was somehow still in the tunnel created by the maskhål, and that's why everything sounded like faint and fading echoes. Was this her world? If it was, why did it feel so strange?

CHAPTER NINE

Ava hated the hot chocolate from the food court. So of course, that's what Tricia brought her.

Tricia set it down on the vast desk that occupied nearly half her office. There was a crack in the glass top that had been mended with a thick band of epoxy, and Ava found her eyes tracing its length as Tricia made her way to the other side. Everything in this place was so ugly.

Tricia cleared her throat. "It seems like you were successful in retrieving Mrs. Nouri."

Ava glanced up at her. She recognized one of Tricia's patented Managerial Faces: Empathetically Dealing With Conflict. "Ursula Nouri got eaten by a plant," Ava said. "That's her 'appropriate replacement.'"

Tricia's Managerial Face cracked into a frown. "I see. Well, the EMTs told me that she was seriously injured, but will likely recover."

"Did they say where they were taking her?" asked Ava. Her eyes drifted back to the epoxied crack in the glass.

"Saint Joseph's Hospital, I believe."

Ava nodded. There was a long, heavy silence. Then she

said, "Jules isn't coming back."

She wasn't sure what she expected. Tricia to swear, fume, roll her eyes. Make a cutting, disparaging remark, at the very least, about Jules's unreliability.

Instead, Tricia nodded again. "I understand."

Ava flicked her eyes up from the crack, boring into Tricia. "Do you."

Tricia transitioned smoothly into the Blank Wall. "What a loss," she said. "Jules was a great employee."

She thought Jules was dead, Ava realized.

Tricia pulled open one of the desk drawers, fished some papers out of it, and slid them across the desk. "I've got some additional paperwork I'll need you to fill out, detailing the incident for internal records and for OSHA—"

"They're not—" Ava couldn't bring herself to say "dead," not even to deny it. Her throat locked up around the word. "Jules stayed behind."

"Oh!" Tricia said. "Oh, that's fantastic! So much less paperwork if Jules just walked off the job."

She smiled at Ava, like it was a joke they were sharing in.

"Jules never just walked away from anything," Ava hissed. "They hated this job and LitenVärld and all the suburbanites bitching about their wedding registries, and they still dragged themself in here." She leaned back in her chair, taking a deep, petty pleasure in the fact that she'd managed to cut through all of Tricia's prepared remarks and expressions. "They deserve better than this place, and I hope they . . ."

Her thoughts suddenly derailed. Whatever she hoped for Jules didn't matter. She didn't actually know if they'd survived.

Tricia was silent for several seconds before letting out a slow, calming breath. "I understand this was a stressful shift for you," she said. "Why don't you take the rest of the day off? You've got some PTO saved up, I think."

Ava repressed the urge to scream. "Can I just get a couple minutes alone?" she asked.

"Of course," Tricia said. She seemed smug now. "You're overdue for a ten-minute break. Enjoy your hot chocolate while it's still warm."

She got up, came around the desk, and seemed to hesitate by Ava's side. Ava, the aftertaste of rage thick in her mouth, decided that if Tricia touched her—gave her a supporting pat on the shoulder or, god forbid, *tried to hug her*—that she would not feel even a bit guilty for punching her manager right in the face. Maybe Tricia sensed that, maybe she just remembered it was time for her own lunch break. Regardless, she moved past and toward the door, where she paused.

"Oh," she said, turning back. "I will need the FINNA back from you."

Ava clenched her jaw. "I lost it in the last wormhole," she said. She gestured to her tunic, which didn't have pockets. "I was a little preoccupied with getting through the maskhål before it collapsed and trapped me in the void."

Tricia huffed a short, sharp sigh of annoyance. "Corporate is *not* going to like that. I have some calls to make." She put on the Not Angry, Just Disappointed face. "I'll let you know what they say."

The office door clicked softly shut behind her.

Ava slumped forward. She clasped her hands around her elbows and hunched over, shuddering uncontrollably. "Shit, shit, *shit.*"

She had left Jules behind. She had no idea if they were alive or not. She thought of how she had rushed forward the first time, and had looked back to see Nouresh torn open. What would she have seen if she'd looked back the second time, when Jules had stayed?

There was no way they could have survived the horde. Almost instantaneously, her mind reversed course: *of course* Jules was alive, they had never faced a challenge whose ass they couldn't kick, and they had the stores of righteous rage that all retail employees collected. Reinforcements had been on their way, right? It was impossible to think that Jules was dead. But there were so many

Danas and Marks, how could Jules have survived?

Ava's brain spun in circles, unable to decide if Jules was alive or dead, triumphant or lying in pieces. It was like looking at all the mirrored realities that she'd seen in the collapsing maskhål; but instead of cracking apart, dispersing into the void, these seemed to grow larger, crowd her brain more violently. Alive. Dead. Happy. Dismembered. Alive and celebrating victory. Torn into bloody pieces and cursing Ava with their last breath.

Ava lost minutes to the static in her head, before she could remember how breathing worked and how to move her limbs. She was left with the overwhelming urge to sleep, to stress-nap away the next several hours. She briefly thought of her favorite LitenVärld cube for illicit naps, the Goth Spinster room that was draped in black and velvet. But even that made her shudder. More than anything, Ava realized, she wanted to get the hell out of this store.

And she never wanted to come back.

Her legs felt like rubber when she stood, but held her weight after a few wobbly steps. She made her way out of Tricia's office, then into the break room. She grabbed the coat out of her locker, her hat and gloves, and was about to shut it again when her eyes drifted to Jules's locker.

Back when they'd first started dating, the two of them would leave silly, stupid notes in each other's lockers.

Jules occasionally folded theirs into complicated origami: whales, giraffes, penguins. Ava had saved them, of course. After the breakup she'd shoved them all into a shoebox, along with all of the other detritus and memorabilia from their relationship.

Ava pulled open Jules's locker, crouching in front of it to look inside. She was first confronted by a bunch of dirty lunch containers, of course. Ava had to laugh, because honestly, Jules was such a slob about some shit. Some unopened granola bars. Their winter coat, an old dumpy thing that they'd bought from a Goodwill ages ago.

And, hiding at the back, the scarf that Ava had made for them. She remembered the sight of it around their throat that morning, how it had made her stomach churn and acid sting her throat.

Ava pulled it out gingerly past the granola bars and molding Tupperware, as if it were liable to explode. She looked at it, rubbing her thumbs against the tightly knit wool. The hope she'd poured into it hadn't worked the way she'd imagined. She and Jules were never going to be a couple again, but—what was it Nouresh had called it? They could have found their footing with one another. Knit themselves back together in a different shape.

She briefly felt the urge to make a big exit. Destroy the break room, flip a table, light Tricia's desk on fire, pull the alarm. The urge passed; she was too damn tired for the melodrama. She settled for writing "I QUIT" on her ID card in permanent marker and leaving it artfully draped across the hot chocolate she hadn't drunk. Then she took the back stairs out to the loading dock, where the half-dozen dudes paid her no more mind than they ever had, and walked the three-quarters of a mile to the bus stop.

She dozed off on the bus, missed her stop, but recognized where she was and pulled the cord. The bus let her off about a mile from Jules's studio apartment, which had, for a brief couple of months, been nearly as familiar as her own home. Ava trundled slowly through the snow, which had continued to spit down through the day, spiteful and cold, turning the sidewalk treacherous. The mile-long walk took nearly twice as long as normal, with the road slippery and arduous. Ava pulled the scarf tighter across her face as the wind slapped bits of ice into her eyes and cheeks.

The spare key, thankfully, was exactly where she remembered it, under the novelty welcome mat that said *Hello . . . Is it me you're looking for?* If they were here, she would have yelled at Jules for not moving the key, hiding it better. *Who's going to break into a shitty third-floor attic apartment with a Lionel Richie mat?* they always said. *Besides, I got fuck-all worth stealing. The most expensive shit I've got in there is the coffee my parents buy me.*

Ava slipped the key into the deadbolt and unlocked the door. Jules's coffee was really good. Better than the shit she bought.

It was warm inside, because Jules tended to run cold. Ava let herself in, toeing off her shoes and dropping her coat onto an empty hook. Jules's studio should have looked different; so much had changed since Ava had been here last, though that had only been about a week ago. But no, there was the same rickety bed pushed up against the wall. Same dresser, half the drawers hanging open, spare change and half-empty water glasses and mugs littering the top. Same bulletin board covered with pictures of places that Jules planned to travel to someday, or that they'd traveled to already. They had left their dishes from breakfast in the sink, which could do with a good scrub, and there were papers and stuff all over the kitchen counters.

Ava absentmindedly tidied up the papers, automatic as breathing. She'd always been picking up Jules's apartment, since the mess made her itch. She wasn't really looking at what she was picking up, not really, until she noticed her own name at the top of a page.

Dear Ava,

~~*You once told me that*~~

Nothing else was written below it.

Ava dropped the paper back on the counter, then sat on the bed. Her mind felt . . . blank. Heavy. Like it had been filled with the same epoxy that had been poured into the crack in Tricia's desk.

Ava pulled off the clothes she'd bought in that market—had it only been a couple hours ago? It felt like months—kicked them onto the floor, and curled up under Jules's duvet. She was asleep almost instantly, and stayed that way for nearly fifteen hours, dreaming that she had traveled to other worlds, dreaming that she had never left, dreaming that Jules had just stepped out for coffee.

CHAPTER TEN

Two days later, a taxi dropped Ava off in front of Saint Joseph's. The enormous edifice reminded her of the *L. V. Anahita* when it had surfaced beneath them: too big to understand, to hold entirely in her mind. She almost got back in the car, the request to take her home on her lips. Then she shook herself and went inside, following the complicated directions to Ursula Nouri's room in the recovery unit. She'd timed her arrival to coincide with the beginning of visiting hours, but it took her nearly half an hour to find the correct floor, and then the correct room. Customers at LitenVärld complained about getting lost in the store, unable to find their bearings. Ava had felt the same when she'd first been hired, but it was even worse at the hospital, which felt like a labyrinth by comparison.

Ava sighed in relief when she finally spotted the paper plaque with the name *Nouri* on it. She raised her hand to knock, put it down, shook herself. Why was she so nervous? She'd carried this woman barely conscious through a tunnel in time and space. A fifteen-minute conversation wasn't too much to ask. She rapped on the door.

It opened, after a moment, to reveal the young woman who had come to the customer service desk in the first place. Ursula's granddaughter. She stared blankly at Ava until recognition washed over her face. "Hi!" she said. "Sorry, come in. Grandma, look who it is!"

Ava blinked at the sight of Captain Nouresh in the hospital bed; she looked smaller without her imposing coat and sword. She seemed paler, as well, either from blood loss or from the gray February light filtering through the window. Bulky bandages peeked out from the neck of her hospital gown, and wound around her arms.

Still, her eyes were lively and sharp as they alighted on Ava. She shifted a bit, sitting up with a pained grunt. "Hello, hero," she said. "I hear I owe you some gratitude."

"Grandma, use the buttons on the bed to sit up," the girl fussed. She adjusted the pillows propping Nouresh up, and said, "Sorry, I don't think we've properly met. I'm Farah."

"Ava," she replied, and they shook hands.

"I don't know if thanking you is like, even appropriate?" Farah said. "But holy shit, thank you so much."

Ava, unnerved by the girl's sincerity, muttered, "It's fine, really, I—"

"Are you a hugger? Do you hug?"

Ava looked over at Nouresh helplessly, and the older

woman shrugged, then winced as she pulled at her wound.

"Sure?" Ava said. Before she could prepare herself, Farah's arms were around her, squeezing her fiercely. It was sort of alarming, really.

Farah released her, but only long enough to plant a kiss on each of Ava's cheeks. "If you need anything—like, seriously, *anything*—I will help you."

Ava nodded, quailing under Farah's intent gaze. She was a lot more like Nouresh than seemed possible.

"Farah, dear, could you get us some tea? Maybe give us some time to talk?" Nouresh asked.

Farah nodded, then looked back at Ava. "Make sure she doesn't wander off, okay?"

Ava nodded again, and Nouresh added, "We'll keep each other firmly on this earth." Farah squeezed Ava's hand once, with a terrifying strength, and then went out into the hallway, shutting the door behind her.

"She seems . . . cool," Ava said after a moment.

"She does, doesn't she?" Nouresh said. Her voice was fond, a little surprised. "I wasn't sure what to expect, but her grandmother raised her well."

"Pour one out for Ursula," Ava said.

"May the sea keep her memory," Nouresh agreed.

"How much does Farah know?" Ava asked delicately. "About what happened?"

Nouresh pursed her lips. "She's chalking some of what I said up to a concussion. To be fair, I said most of it when I was barely conscious . . ." She sighed. "But it hasn't escaped her notice that her beloved grandmother has many more scars and significantly longer hair."

"Are you going to tell her?"

"Eventually," Nouresh said. "She deserves that. Ursula does as well."

Ava sat in the chair by the bed. It was comfortingly warm; Farah must have been sitting there. "Captain Nouresh," she started.

The older woman raised a hand. "You carried me through a collapsing marejii, I think you've earned the right to call me Uzmala."

Ava nodded. "Uzmala. Do you remember what happened to Jules?"

Uzmala sighed. "I know they saved my life. I know they pulled me through that door. It gets hazy after that. Farah told me that the two of us emerged alone."

Ava chewed on her lip. "Jules stayed behind. They held the door. I think they fought the drones."

"A good place to make a stand," Uzmala mused. "Those bulkhead doors are narrow, and they would have had to come through one at a time. Someone handy with a sword could hold off a horde for quite a while."

Ava's stomach roiled. She'd forced herself to go back to

her own apartment the night before, to eat and to gather the things she'd thought she needed. Her meal sat uneasily in her stomach now, and she had to swallow a couple times before she could speak the question she'd come here to ask: "I don't suppose you still have your coat, do you?"

Uzmala smiled at her. "They bagged all my belongings and left them in the closet in the corner. What you're looking for should be in there."

Ava got up, pulled the red plastic bag from the closet, and tore it open with shaking fingers, even though she could already feel the FINNA's bulky shape through the thin plastic. Ava only had dim memories of running through the last maskhål, but she clearly remembered slipping the FINNA into the wide pocket of Uzmala's red coat, worried that it would slip from her sweaty hands. Uzmala had still been wearing the coat when the ambulance crew strapped her to the stretcher, and Ava had been hustled off to the break room.

The coat was stiff with dried blood, but she was able to maneuver the FINNA out of the pocket. She carefully put the bag back in the closet and then sat back down by Uzmala's bedside.

"Did I mention that I quit my job?" Ava said faintly.

"Good for you," the older woman replied. "I might be biased because I was dying at the time, but that store seemed like a depressing place to spend your hours."

"It's only the second job I've ever had," Ava said. "My boss, Tricia, always said that we were a family. I should have realized she meant that I would have to put up with constant bullshit."

Uzmala nodded, though she winced as she did, and put a hand up to her bandaged shoulder. "Was my tool bag in the closet? Fetch it for me, will you?"

Ava did, laying it gently on Uzmala's lap. "Give me that thing," Uzmala said, holding her free hand out for the FINNA. After a brief hesitation, Ava did so.

"Correct me if I'm wrong, but it sounds like you have nothing really holding you here. And one compelling reason to leave," Uzmala said, popping the back of the FINNA open. "Not to mention a good vehicle out. This thing is old, but hardy."

"You would know, right?" Ava said weakly. "Being old and hardy yourself?"

There was a hint of steel in Uzmala's eyes as the woman looked at her, unimpressed. Ava shrank back in her chair.

"Anyway," Uzmala said. "What's holding you back?"

"You mean besides the monsters that nearly ate us?" Ava shot back.

Uzmala fished a thin, copper-and-steel screwdriver out of her tool bag. "Every world has its monsters. I've been watching the news, and yours is no exception. What's the real reason?"

Ava shut her eyes. She didn't want to say it; saying it made it real, instead of just a nebulous, nightmarish fear inside her head. Then she thought of the two lines in an unfinished letter, and all the things that she and Jules might never say to each other.

"What if I tell the FINNA to find Jules," she said slowly, quietly. "And it says they're . . . indisposed? Like Ursula was?"

The look that Uzmala gave her this time was longer, softer, and more thoughtful.

"Don't get me wrong," Ava said, "I'm glad that you and Farah are doing okay, but I don't want an *appropriate replacement* for Jules."

"Even if the alternative is never to see them again?" There was no judgment in the question, just a soft understanding. Ava remembered Nouresh's sad smile, back at the *Anahita*'s bazaar, when Ava asked the captain if she had a family. *Not anymore.*

But this wasn't the same, was it? She didn't *know* if Jules was dead. They were Schrödinger's Cat at this point, alive and dead and all points in between until Ava made a choice to find out. And if they were alive? What then? It was hard to articulate what Ava wanted, even to herself. She didn't want to find Jules and run straight back into their arms. But she'd felt something new growing between them, something fragile but important. And she wanted to protect that, nourish it, and see it mature.

Uzmala waited her out, not pressuring her to answer, just patiently poking around in the FINNA. Ava watched her careful, precise movements with a sort of distant focus, thinking about Nouresh's question.

"I want to know if they're okay," Ava answered finally. "Everything after that is negotiable."

Uzmala nodded. She worked in silence on the FINNA, examining it with steady, sure movements, for a few moments before asking, "You know what I loved about traveling by marejii?"

It took Ava a second to catch up with the conversation. "No, what?"

"It showed me that there were infinite possibilities, at all times. After I made captain of the *Anahita,* I worried over every decision, doubted whether I was brave or smart or strong enough to pull my mission off and protect my crew. I could remind myself that somewhere in the multiverse of possibility, there existed a world where I was all of those things. Maybe it was the world that I already lived in."

She bent her head closer to the FINNA, then used a delicate pair of pliers to yank something out: it looked like a cross between a computer chip and a spider, and

Ava pushed back in her chair as it gave a weak twitch. It had the LitenVärld logo on it.

"There you are, you bastard," Uzmala said, smiling grimly at it. She dropped it on the bedside table. The thing tried to skitter away, pulling itself along with its two front legs, though it didn't get far. Uzmala stabbed it with the pliers still in her hand, cracking it into pieces. There was a wisp of bright, sky-blue dust, which dispersed almost instantly.

"That should make things easier," Uzmala said. She slid the cover back onto the FINNA and screwed it shut.

"What did you do?" Ava asked.

"I freed it to call up marejii in any labyrinth, not just ones that are analogous to your former job. Anywhere that gets you disoriented enough so that the walls between universes are not so firm can hide a marejii." She gestured to the room around them. "This hospital would probably work. I almost perished of hunger just trying to find the damned toilet down the hall."

She held the FINNA out to Ava, who reached cautiously for it. At the last second, Uzmala pulled it back.

"Now the way I see it," she said, "there are infinite universes where Jules died. And infinite universes where they're alive. Similarly, there are worlds where you are too much of a coward to find out, and worlds where you are brave enough. So. It's up to you: which of those worlds do we exist in right now?"

• • •

As she walked the hospital's twisting hallways, a curious feeling came over Ava; that she almost didn't need the FINNA. To go where she wanted, she had to get lost, and it seemed almost instinctual to do that now. She'd been lost for a long time, rudderless.

Still, she wasn't so brave or so stupid as to rely on instincts alone. She looked back down at the FINNA. The bubble, where she'd placed a tassel cut from the scarf she'd knitted for Jules, glowed a bright, verdant green. The color seemed appropriate: something new, different, and just beginning to grow.

Ava chased that particular sense of disorientation, recognizable now; somewhere between the feeling of falling in love and falling out of it, of pursuing and fleeing, of not knowing and still going forward. Ahead of her, she saw the crackling energy of a split in the world she knew, a doorway into a world that she didn't. Ava ran through it and kept running.

Acknowledgments

First and foremost, thanks to my agent, DongWon Song, who helped maneuver this book into Tor's hands, where I always hoped it would be. Carl Engle-Laird is a fantastic editor, and was infinitely patient when I was editing this in between teaching and defending my thesis. Much gratitude to the team at Tor.com for their hard work, including Irene Gallo, Christine Foltzer, Mordicai Knode, Caroline Perny, and Amanda Melfi.

Lara Elena Donnelly gave me the premise for this story when she had the perfect answer to "Where would a wormhole in IKEA lead to?"

This story was originally written as a screenplay for Darren Canady's workshop at the University of Kansas. It was shaped by his brilliant feedback, and by my classmates'.

Nibedita Sen is the best human, you will not change my mind. She made sure I had adequate caffeine, water, and snugs to finish the initial draft, and told me never to start a story with a character being sad and mopey on a bus. She is very wise.

Karin Tidbeck was my Swedish consultant and came

up with the name for the FINNA. Mar Romasco Moore and Meg Ellison were amazing beta readers, and Rivers Solomon provided a stellar and insightful sensitivity read. Birch Harlen and Jay Wolf helped me come up with fake corporate brands, and Birch is responsible for Pasta and Friends, which is perfectly loathsome.

Jessica Fujan and Zoë Lukens helped me survive my first-ever trip to IKEA. k8 Walton helped me survive, period.

I would not be here, be me, or be writing without my mom, Ellen, or my sibling, Leah.

This book is dedicated to my grandmothers: Phyllis Simons, Vera Anderson, and Elma Connolly, whom I love dearly and miss deeply. I wish they were alive to see their names written here. I am so lucky to have shared as many years as I did with them.

Lastly, Ursula K. Le Guin's work opened a lot of doorways in my imagination, and she reminded us all that the paradigms of power are neither inescapable nor omnipotent. We can imagine better alternatives.

About the Author

NINO CIPRI is a queer and trans/nonbinary writer, editor, and educator. They are a graduate of the Clarion Writing Workshop and the University of Kansas's MFA program, and author of the award-winning debut fiction collection *Homesick* (2019) and the novella *Finna* (2020). Nino has also written plays, poetry, and radio features; performed as a dancer, actor, and puppeteer; and worked as a stagehand, bookseller, bike mechanic, and labor organizer. One time, an angry person on the internet called Nino a verbal terrorist, which was pretty funny. You can talk to Nino on Facebook or Twitter @ninocipri, or on their website, ninocipri.com.

TOR·COM

**Science fiction. Fantasy. The universe.
And related subjects.**

*

More than just a publisher's website, *Tor.com*
is a venue for **original fiction, comics,** and
discussion of the entire field of SF and fantasy,
in all media and from all sources. Visit our site
today—and join the conversation yourself.

Printed in the USA
CPSIA information can be obtained
at www.ICGtesting.com
LVHW051039081223
765932LV00002B/269

9 781250 245731